I rack my brain for some truths and a lie about me. I decide to take a page from Amber's book and keep it simple and boring. "I've never played basketball in my life, I'm an only child, I don't like chocolate, my favorite color is purple, and . . ." I try to come up with one more truth about myself.

But before I can, Crissa chimes in. " . . . and you came here for a really mysterious reason that you don't want anyone to know about?"

An awkward silence falls across the group. I can feel everyone's eyes on me, and the air suddenly feels thick, like a rubber band is squeezing the room.

Also available
from Lauren Barnholdt:

❤ ❤ ❤

*The Secret Identity
of Devon Delaney*

Four Truths and a Lie

LAUREN BARNHOLDT

ALADDIN MIX
NEW YORK   LONDON   TORONTO   SYDNEY

For Aaron, who always believes in me,
even when I don't believe in myself.
I am so lucky to have you in my life.

m!x

ALADDIN MIX
1230 Avenue of the Americas, New York, NY 10020
Text copyright © 2008 by Lauren Barnholdt
All rights reserved, including the right of reproduction in whole or in part in any form.
ALADDIN PAPERBACKS, ALADDIN MIX, and related logo are registered trademarks of Simon & Schuster, Inc.
Designed by Mike Rosamilia
The text of this book was set in Cochin.
Manufactured in the United States of America
First Aladdin Mix edition September 2008
10 9 8 7 6
Library of Congress Control Number 2007943605
ISBN-13: 978-1-4169-3504-9
ISBN-10: 1-4169-3504-5

I'm all about new experiences. Like last year, in seventh grade, when we got to do step aerobics in gym class. And everyone else was complaining, because they thought step aerobics wasn't that fun and made you all sweaty, but I was glad for the change. Or a couple summers ago, when I got to go white-water rafting with my dad. It was scary at times, and of course I got super wet when the raft flipped over, but it was also fun, *and* I got some very cool pictures to bring in for "What Did You Do on Your Summer Vacation?"

But I like to be able to *pick* my new experiences. I don't do well with things that are chosen for me. Like my new school uniform, for example.

"You'll look adorable," my mom says, like she's talking about bathing suits for some great vacation on a Caribbean island, instead of the Brookline Academy for Girls uniform. Which, FYI, is a ridiculous-looking plaid skirt (red, blue, white, and LONG), and a heavy white shirt with a huge collar. The whole thing is very shapeless and will not match any of my shoes, including the pair I just bought: ultrafab Christian Louboutins with a chunky heel.

"I will not look adorable," I say. "I'm going to look like a complete fool. I thought private school uniforms were supposed be cute." It's my first day here, and we're walking up to my room on the third floor. The elevator is apparently broken, so I'm being forced to carry my bag up three flights of stairs. Every time I move up a step, my suitcase bangs against my leg. *Bang.* I wonder if I could cut the skirt a few inches. *Bang.* Or wear a pink shirt with it instead of white. *Bang.* Or maybe I could make a cute dress out of the whole uniform, as long as I kept the pattern. *Bang, bang, bang.* Who ever heard of an elevator being broken on move-in day, anyway? This doesn't seem like a very good start.

"Here we are!" my mom says. "Room three fourteen!"

There are two construction-paper cutouts on the door, one blue, one pink. They're in the shape of guitars, and my name, Scarlett, is written on the blue one, and my roommate's name, Crissa, is written on the pink one. The Brookline Academy is an all-girls school. Why would they have pink and *blue* cutouts? And how come I got stuck with the blue one? Everyone knows pink's my fave color. I wrote it down on my new-student questionnaire and everything.

I push past my mom into the room. It's cute, with two twin beds by the window, two desks, and two small closets. Two *very* small closets. Wow. Why would they make the closets so small? And how am I going to fit all my clothes in there? Did the architects not realize that girls would be living here? Probably they thought it would be fine, since we'd be wearing our uniforms all the time.

"I hope there's not a fire," my mom's saying, looking out the window nervously.

"There won't be a fire," I tell her. I plop myself down on one of the twin beds by the window. I think maybe I need a nap. Starting a new school is stressful.

"Well, I'm sure they'll go over all the emergency routes with you at orientation," my mom says. "And there's a fire escape."

"Yeah, good thing," I say. "Although I hope no one climbs up it. That would really suck, an intruder coming in by using what is supposed to be a life-saving mechanism."

"We should probably start making your bed," she says,

ignoring me and reaching into one of my bags. She pulls out two packages of sheets, one red, and one white with blue flowers. "Which ones do you want?"

"Red." I pull myself off the bed and sigh. There's a stack of boxes in the middle of the room — stuff we had shipped here last week. My roommate's stuff (Crissa, I guess, according to the cutout on the door) is there too, although from the looks of it, she doesn't have as much as I do.

I hate unpacking. I open a box marked BOOKS and start shoving them haphazardly on the shelf over my desk. I actually have a surprising number of books, although I like to read romance novels, so I don't think this is going to gain me any points here. Probably all the girls here read Shakespeare. And Hemingway. And that one *War and Peace* book that's supposedly like a bazillion pages long. Not that there's anything wrong with these books, I'm sure. But I'll bet they don't have any good happy endings, like in *The Duke's Kiss*, this one really good book where the duke and this normal girl spend the whole time trying to overcome social barriers before they finally get together.

Brookline is a charter boarding school that was started by my mom's best friend and college roommate, this woman named Marion O'Neal. Basically it's for really smart girls. Their motto is "Fine young women, excellent head starts."

Yikes. You have to take this supercompetitive placement test just to get in—well, I didn't have to take the test, which was a good thing, because I probably wouldn't have passed it.

But it's fine, since I totally have a plan for how to come off as smart.

This includes, but is not limited to, the following:

1. Do not let ANYONE find out the real reason I am here, i.e., very big scandal involving my dad, which made me have to leave my old school due to general disgrace and losing all my friends. Once people find this out, they will realize I am not smart. Not to mention they will want to talk about said scandal, and will probably (definitely) gossip behind my back.

2. Act smart. One time I watched this show about how just presenting a certain attitude totally made people think you were whatever you were pretending to be. So I'm going to act smart. I even bought a pair of fake glasses (Chanel, black spectacles, totally cute.)

3. Work hard. This is going to be the hardest one, since I'm not so good at doing things that require, um, well, work. But I know I'm going to have to apply myself. Plus, even though I was allowed in here and everything, if I don't keep my average at a B or better, we'll have to "revisit the situation." That's what Headmistress O'Neal told me when they let me in. "Revisit the situation." I'm

determined that I will not be revisiting anything while I'm here.
Not my grades, and certainly not my past.

I'm debating whether or not I should just hide all my
romance novels under my bed when a girl walks into my
room.

"Hello," she says from the doorway. I'm so startled I
drop *The Duke's Kiss* right on the ground.

"Oh," I say, picking it up and shoving it back in the box.
"Hey."

She comes over and sets her suitcase carefully down on
the other bed, then holds her hand out to me. "I'm Crissa."
She has long, smooth, brown hair, and she's wearing jeans
and a T-shirt that says I ♥ NY. There's a black messenger bag
slung over her shoulder.

"Nice to meet you," I say, taking Crissa's hand and
shaking it. "I'm Scarlett." Yay for roommates! At first I was
a little nervous about having to share a room with someone.
I'm an only child and I've always had my own room. But
now I'm totally into the idea. Staying up all night talking
and gossiping. Reading magazines and doing each other's
hair. Watching movies and eating —

"I see you've already picked your bed." Crissa thrusts
her chin in the air.

"Oh, um, yeah." Ooopsies. I just figured whoever gets here first gets first pick of the beds. That's how they do it on all those reality shows. Of course, a big fight usually ensues after that, but still. "I hope that's okay."

She shrugs. The door to our room flies open again, and a gray-haired woman in a blue dress appears. "Honestly, Crissa," she says. "You didn't have to run up the stairs. You know I have a bad knee." She smoothes her hair. "It wouldn't hurt you to act like a lady."

"Sorry, Mother," Crissa says. She heads over to the other bed, and drops her bag on it.

"Hello," the woman says, looking me up and down. "I'm Crissa's mom, Debbie Bacon." She frowns, and her eyebrows wrinkle. "*Mrs*. Bacon." I try not to burst out laughing. Bacon. Ha-ha. But then I realize she made a big point of making sure I knew to call her Mrs. Bacon, and it's not really that funny anymore. Does she think I'm some kind of delinquent?

"Pleased to meet you," I say. For a second, I think maybe I should curtsy or something, but then I realize I'm not wearing my uniform yet. From behind me, my mom clears her throat. "Oh, I'm sorry." I look from Crissa and Mrs. Bacon to my mom. "This is my mom, Mrs. Northon."

"Nice to meet you," my mom says.

We all stare at each other awkwardly for a moment.

"So the headmistress tells me you're a transfer from Rockville Public," Mrs. Bacon says. There's a smile on her lips, but it's not quite reaching her eyes. And the way she says "Rockville Public" makes it sound really bad, like anyone who comes from public school is two seconds away from ending up on the streets. Which isn't true. I mean, Rockville Public is in the richest district in Massachusetts.

"Yes," my mom says, standing up and putting her hands on my shoulder. "We thought Scarlett would benefit from a more challenging academic environment." Wow. Way to go, Mom.

"Mmmm," Mrs. Bacon says. "Challenging it certainly is." She glances at her watch. "I don't mean to be rude, but I'm terribly late for my steering committee," she says. Steering committee? Is Mrs. Bacon a race car driver? "Now, Crissa, please make sure you let me know when you find out who you have for math." She tightens the scarf around her neck. "And if there's any problem with the gray knee socks, please call me immediately." She kisses both of Crissa's cheeks, says good-bye to me and my mom, and then disappears out the door. Ooo-kay, then.

Crissa says nothing. Maybe she's just nervous around parents. That happens to me sometimes, like when my friend (well, I guess ex-friend now since no one from my old school will talk to me) Taylor had a pool party and her mom kept asking all the girls if they were looking forward to starting eighth grade and who was the hottest boy in school. It was quite unnerving and very annoying. I shoot my mom a pointed look, which basically means, *If you want me to have any friends here, you should probably leave. Like now. I don't want to be the lame girl whose mom is hanging around her on the first day of school.*

"Well," my mom says, getting the hint. She checks her watch and stands up. "I should probably get going too." I can tell she wants to say something else, but not in front of Crissa. "Call me tonight if you need anything."

"Of course," I say, rolling my eyes to show Crissa that I'm not worried about it. No getting homesick for me, definitely not. Never mind that I've never spent any significant amount of time away from home, and never really liked sleepovers.

"So," Crissa says, once my mom's gone. Her brown eyes look me up and down. "I heard you only got in here because your mom knows Headmistress O'Neal."

"Oh," I say, taken aback. I reach into the box of books and pull out two more, then shove them onto the shelf. "Yeah. Well, I'm not, um . . ." Crap. I didn't come prepared with a cover story. Maybe I can tell everyone I got kicked out of my old school for fighting or something—I always wanted to be a tough girl. "I'm not really supposed to talk about it," I say, hoping she gets the hint.

"What's that supposed to mean?" She opens her suitcase, removes a gray cardigan sweater, slides it on, and begins to button it up very carefully. Then she takes out a picture frame and places it on her nightstand. It's a silver frame, with swirly black letters all over it, spelling out "friends," "best friends forever," and "love." In it, there's a picture of Crissa with another girl, their arms around each other, smiling into the camera.

"Um, well," I say slowly, trying to keep my voice light. "My mom thought it would be good for me." Which is true. Crissa raises her eyebrows, which need serious tweezing. "Cool picture," I say, trying to change the subject. "Who is it?" I pick up the frame and study the picture.

"My best friend," Crissa says, taking the picture out of my hand and placing it back on the nightstand. "Her name's Marissa. She was my roommate last year, and she was *supposed* to be my roommate this year, but she moved. She goes to school in California now."

"She looks nice," I say.

"She's amazing," Crissa says. "We totally ruled this school."

Jeez. Way to be obvious. Okay, so maybe I'm not Marissa. But that doesn't mean me and Crissa can't be friends, right? I mean, I can be as cool as Marissa. I can smile into the camera and rule the school with Crissa, right? Although we're obviously not off to a very good start.

My thoughts are interrupted by squeals coming from our doorway. The squeals are coming from two girls, one with mopsy brown hair, and a blonde with large red-framed glasses. (Ha! I knew glasses would be popular around here.) Crissa jumps off the bed and runs to the girls—and they all embrace and jump around.

Well. She's obviously a little warmer to them than she was to me.

"I can't believe you cut your hair!" Crissa says to the blond one. "Does it feel weird, it being so short?" That's what she calls short? It's halfway down the girl's back.

"Not really," the girl says, tossing her hair around.

"I love it," Crissa says. "It suits your face."

"I'm so sorry about . . ." the blonde trails off and gives Crissa a sympathetic look, then squeezes her shoulder. "I hope you're okay."

"I'm so fine it's ridiculous," Crissa says. "I mean, it was my choice."

"Is your mom freaking out?" the blonde says. I have

no idea what they're talking about, so I can't even get in on the gossip.

"Kind of," Crissa says. She looks uncomfortable. "But it's really not her decision."

"Oh," the brunette says, looking over Crissa's shoulder. "Is this your new roommate?"

"Yeah," Crissa says, as if she forgot I was sitting there. Maybe I should have worn my fake glasses right off the bat. I wonder if it would be too obvious to go searching through my bag and pull them out. I could be all, "Look! I found my glasses, whew, much better. I totally need them when I read my copy of *War and Peace*, the print is so small."

"Scarlett," Crissa says, "this is Tia"—the brunette—"and Rachel."—the blonde.

Upon further inspection, Tia and Rachel would benefit from my tweezers just as much as Crissa would. And then I have a brilliant idea. I could do makeovers! My heart starts to rise a little bit as I think about the possibilities. I could take these three under my wing, turning them from ugly ducklings into swans! And then the four of us would become the most popular girls in school, totally taking out the current most popular girls in school, who have always (of course) been mean to them in the past! And it would be way better than anything Crissa had with Marissa. It would be like a Disney movie, only better because it would be my life! And sure, it won't *really* be the same, since there aren't any boys here (everyone knows that in these movies, the popular boys fall in love with the newly made-over girls), but still.

"Nice to meet you," Rachel says.

Tia just looks me up and down.

"Nice to meet you both," I say, making a big production of pulling out my makeup bag. "Does anyone want any"—I pause for effect—"Kiehl's products?"

I expect this announcement to be met with squeals of excitement, and then a trip down the hall to the (communal, eww) bathrooms for facials and fun. But they all just stare at me blankly.

"It's okay," I say. "I don't mind sharing. We can do facials!"

"What are Keels?" Crissa peers over at my bed for a closer look. Is she kidding? *What are Kiehl's?*

"They're product," I say. "Skin stuff. You know, for facials?"

"Ooooh," Rachel says, nodding. "My sister gets those."

"Let's go do facials," I say. "I have exfoliator, a mud mask, a—"

"We can't," Tia says, speaking to me for the first time. "We have to sign up for extras."

"Extras?" I ask.

"Extracurriculars," Rachel explains. She holds up a jar of moisturizer. "I wonder if this would help my dry skin."

"It totally would," I say. "And this is the lotion that goes with it." I hand her the bottle.

"We *have* to get to extras," Crissa says forcefully. She taps her sneakered foot on our floor. "But maybe later we can play with your *product*." She says "product" as if it's some kind of dirty word. Plus you don't *play* with product. It's not a yo-yo.

Rachel rolls her eyes, and pulls a bag of Swedish fish out of her pocket. She opens them and pops one into her mouth. "Extras don't start for another ten minutes."

"Yeah, but if we don't get there, all the good ones will be taken."

Good ones? There is nothing good about extracurricular activities. Extracurricular means extra—as in after school. Time when you could be doing something else. Like having fun.

"Fine," Rachel says. "Time to go to extras."

"We'd invite you," Crissa says. "But new students have to sign up for extras through their advisor. Sorry." She doesn't look sorry at all.

They file out of the room, leaving me by myself.

I look down at my hands. Whatever. I mean, they can't be the *only* girls here. There are tons of students in my class. Well, okay, like a hundred and fifty. But still. Three out of a hundred and fifty is like . . . Um. Well, it's not a huge percentage. Like, 2 or 3 percent, I think. I've never been good at math. And what was it my mom said? That it would only take one or two really good friends for me to start feeling comfortable? She's totally right.

And besides, after what happened to me at my old school, this is nothing.

I gather up my Kiehl's products and get ready to head to the bathroom. I can give *myself* a facial. It will cheer me up. And maybe while I'm in the bathroom, I'll find another girl there, giving *herself* a facial, and she'll be all, "Oh, hi, I'm so glad there's finally someone here who understands the value of a good facial!" Cheered by this, I grab my facial bag, and then go digging in my luggage for a towel.

I don't need friends to do a facial. Take that, Crissa, with your Tia and your Rachel and your haircuts and your gossip I don't know about. And your probing, sort of inappropriate questions and your—

"Hi!" a voice screeches from the doorway. I drop a tube of moisturizer on the ground and it goes rolling under my bed. What is up with people just appearing out of nowhere in this place? I feel like I'm at Hogwarts.

"Oh," I say. "Uh, hi." I get down on my knees and reach under the bed, groping around for the tube. Eww. It's kind of gross down here. You'd think since it's the first day of school the rooms would be a little cleaner.

The girl (woman?) standing in front of me looks like she's about twenty-five, with long blond hair and green eyes. "You must be Scarlett," she says. "I'm Miss Cardanelli, the eighth-grade English teacher, and also your academic advisor."

"Yes," I say, "I'm Scarlett. And it's nice to meet you." This whole boarding school thing is weird. I mean, having a teacher in your room? Strange. What if I have something embarrassing in here? Like all the romance novels I brought, for example. I definitely don't want my English teacher seeing my romance novels. (Note to self: Buy Shakespeare plays and keep them in room. And definitely find those glasses.)

Miss Cardanelli plops down on Crissa's bed. "So where's Crissa?"

"She went to sign up for extras." I slip the Kiehl's back into my makeup case.

"You didn't feel like signing up for extras yet?" Miss Cardanelli's studying herself in the mirror over Crissa's desk. She has what appears to be glitter in her hair. Figures that the one person who's cool around here happens to be a teacher. This place is like bizarro world.

Somehow it seems inappropriate to tell a teacher that I don't plan on joining any kind of activity. Especially if I'm trying to pretend to be smart. "Crissa told me that I have to wait and sign up through my advisor, so . . ."

Miss Cardanelli frowns. "That's not true," she says. "You have to sign up the same as anyone else. She checks her watch. "And you're already ten minutes late, so if I were you, I'd hurry." She jumps off the bed. "Come on," she says. "I'll show you where to go."

Ten minutes later, I am in the student activities center, trying to weasel my way out of a huge disaster.

"You see, I've never actually played basketball before," I say to the woman sitting at the table in front of me. "I'm not sure if I'd be the best *asset* to the team." Plus I don't want to. I hate sports of any kind. This dates back to two unfortunate incidents, both occurring in the fourth grade—one where I got hit in the head with a volleyball, and then another where I tried to hit a softball in the air, and it came back down and hit me in the eye. I had a black eye for six weeks, and the social worker at my school called my mother to confirm there was nothing scandalous going on at our house.

"That's okay!" the woman, who I am now referring to in my mind as Coach Crazy, says, writing my name down on her clipboard. "No experience necessary! Most of the girls are new, especially on the freshman team, mm-hmm, mm-hmmm." She makes a clucking noise with her tongue. The student activities center is filled with folding tables, each set up with a different extracurricular activity. Somehow, as soon as I walked in, I was accosted by this woman, who is apparently in charge of basketball. And apparently, for some ridiculous reason, wants me on her team. Is she blind? I'm wearing a short black skirt over leggings, a lacy button-up shirt, and ballet flats. I do not look in any way, shape, or form, like a basketball player.

"But I'm actually not a freshman," I try. "I'm only in eighth grade, so . . . "

"That's okay," she says. "The freshman team is for eighth AND ninth graders. And we've lost a couple to JV. Now, we'll need your uniform size." I have no idea what she's talking about. Who is JV? And why is he taking her players? Oh. Right. Junior Varsity. There was this totally hot ninth grader on the JV team last year at my old school, and me and my friend Brianna used to go to his games and scream, "Go, Nathan!" even though he had no idea who we were. Quite fun.

Coach Crazy pulls out a measuring tape and comes out from behind the table. She shoves it around my waist. "Hmm, you're a medium." She looks down at her clipboard. "That's probably going to be a problem, since we don't have any mediums available. Budget constraints, you know?" She shrugs as if to say *What can you do?*

"Um, I don't actually need a uniform," I say. "Because I'm not going to be —"

"No, no, it's okay," Coach Crazy says. "We'll just put you in a large, and hope for the best!" She smiles, revealing slightly yellow teeth. Is she kidding? I will certainly not wear something that doesn't fit me and then "hope for the best." It's bad enough I have to wear a school uniform here; I'm not going to voluntarily sign up to wear a basketball uniform that I don't even want and doesn't even fit.

"You're joining basketball?" Crissa is behind me, and when I turn around, I see Rachel and Tia there too. Coach Crazy doesn't even look at them. Why am I the only one she's harassing? Aren't basketball players supposed to be tall? I'm only 5'2", and I drink coffee almost every morning, so I'm sure my growth has been totally stunted.

"No," I say. "I'm not. I'm not really into sports."

"Oh, good," Rachel says. She leans in close to me. "Basketball's the worst. Coach Chambers takes it super serious; she works the team out like they're in the freakin' NBA or something."

I'm not sure what the NBA is. Doesn't it have something to do with guns? No, wait, that's the NRA. No matter. I'm not joining—the basketball team OR the NRA.

"Now, dear," Coach Chambers/Crazy is saying. She hands me a sheaf of papers. I catch a glimpse of the words "Practice Schedule, Including Rules and Regulations" on the top sheet. "Our first practice is tomorrow at three. Make sure you get there a little bit early, since you'll have to change. Now, what would you say your fitness level is?" She purses her lips and poises her pen to write something down on her clipboard.

"I'm not joining," I say, trying to sound firm.

"So around a four, then," Coach Chambers says, marking something down. "No worries, we'll get you in tip-top shape in no time!" Is Coach Chambers deaf as well as blind?

Rachel yanks my arm, pulling me away from her. "What are you doing?" I ask.

"It's the only way," she says simply. Tia nods.

"Coach Chambers is like that," Rachel says. "She's always trying to recruit, since everyone hates basketball." She shifts her bookbag to the other arm. "She probably realized you were new, and decided you'd be an easy mark."

"Well, thanks," I say, sighing in relief. From behind me, I can hear Coach Chambers calling, "If you change your mind, dear, you can always come to the gym tomorrow at three!"

"So what *are* you going to sign up for?" Tia asks. "So far I'm in computer club and soccer."

"She said she doesn't like sports," Crissa says, scowling. She looks at her watch and taps her foot impatiently on the ground.

"Ooh, computer club's the best," Rachel says. "Because you get to spend a lot of time in the computer lab, and usually you can get away with IM'ing."

I weigh the options—able to IM with my friends (not like I really have any left at home, but my mom has IM, and I'm sure some of my soon-to-be new and fabulous friends at Brookline will be around to IM with. Also, if worse comes to worst, I can spend time playing video games or something. Not like I really do that either, but anything sounds better than running around the gym shooting a ball into a hoop for hours) vs. not having to deal with after-school activities.

"Okay," I say. "I'll sign up too." It will be good for my new "I'm totally smart" image—I mean, extracurricular activities? Totally things that a smart person would do.

"Sorry," Crissa says. "But I think it's closed. Probably

because you got here late." She flips her perfect hair over her shoulder and shrugs. I look over to the other side of the room, where the computer club teacher, a friendly-looking woman wearing a pink T-shirt, has placed a small sign on her table that says FULL. I want to point out that the reason I got here late was because she told me I had to wait for my advisor. But I don't.

"They only let a certain number of people in," Tia says. "But you should sign up for soccer. We have a lot of fun, because the practices are so easy. The team totally sucks, and no one cares. We have fun going to games and just riding the bus and messing around."

"Thanks," I say. "But I don't think I'm an extracurricular kind of girl." I wonder why schools don't have after-school clubs with skills we could actually use. Like beauty club or something. Or even auto club. Although I guess the point of extracurriculars isn't to learn a skill. It's more to have fun. But basketball doesn't sound fun. Not at all.

"Well, you have to pick *something,*" Crissa says. She rolls her eyes at me.

"Why?"

"Because you have to have at least one extracurricular," Tia says. "It's a rule."

Extracurriculars are a rule? What kind of place is this?

"Fine," I say. But as I look around, pretty much every single booth has a sign that says FULL. Except for . . . Sigh.

I walk back over dejectedly.

"Now," Coach Crazy says, brandishing her clipboard. "What kind of sneakers do you have?"

"Nikes." Oh, well. At least it will be good exercise.

"Do you have any shampoo I can borrow?" a voice asks from across the shower divider. It's later that night, and I'm attempting to shower in the communal bathrooms. I prefer baths to showers, but there are no bathtubs at Brookline Academy. Not only that, but everyone has to shower in these little stalls, and there's always a million people running in and out of the bathrooms, so it's kind of distracting. Fortunately, there's a small private changing area outside of the actual shower, and I have all my pajama stuff there. I'm going to grab it and get dressed really quickly before I venture out into the open. I've never been one of those girls that just wanders around getting dressed in front of everyone during gym class like it's nothing. I prefer to do my changing with a little privacy.

"Um, sure," I say to the mysterious voice across the divider. I reach into my shower caddy and pull out my bottle of Clinique Extra Body Shampoo. Hmm.

"Do you have flat hair?" I yell over the divider. No sense in giving her a volumizing shampoo if it's just going to make her hair look like a big Brillo pad.

"What?" she asks back.

"You know, do you have flat hair?" Silence. I try to make it easier. "Straight or curly?"

"Curly," she says. She sounds annoyed. "Now do you have any shampoo or what?"

I fish out my Clinique Exceptionally Clean shampoo, and toss that over the divider instead. She'll have me to thank when her curls are beautifully bouncy.

I lean into the hot water while I wait for her to send it back over. Mmm. The water feels fantastic, especially at the end of such a stressful, long day. After extras (and my run-in with Coach Crazy), we had lunch in the dining hall. The food actually wasn't that bad—they have a fully stocked salad bar, and we had lasagna as the main course. Yum. But then Tia told me not to get too excited about the food since they always serve the best food on the first day, just in case any parents stick around. And there *were* some parents who stayed, which made me feel very thankful my mom took off when she did. It's bad enough that I already stick out here, I don't need my mom hanging around making it worse. Plus who knows what kind of things my mom might have said?

She could have let slip the real reason I'm here.

After lunch we had a welcome assembly from the headmistress, which was kind of weird because she's my mom's roommate from college, even though I've never really met her. Just once, I think, when I was a baby. And when I had my interview here last month. Anyway, she gave us all a big rah-rah speech, and then afterward, on her way out of the auditorium, she came up to me and was like, "Hello, Scarlett, nice to see you. Please come to me if you have any questions." And I was sitting with Tia and Rachel and Crissa and they were all looking at me curiously, and then Rachel started to ask me something, but Tia elbowed her to shut up. So I think they were going to ask me what I'm doing here.

"Are you almost done in there?" another voice screeches from outside my shower stall. I guess long showers don't really work when there's always someone waiting. Oopsies.

"Sorry," I say. My bottle of shampoo comes flying back over the divider, almost hitting me in the head. Jeez. Way to be thankful. I pour some out into my hand, quickly shampoo and condition my hair (whoever that was used a LOT of shampoo, like almost the whole bottle, which is pretty rude since it's kind of expensive, but whatev), wrap a towel around my head, and then quickly get into my pajamas.

I don't have time to dry off completely, so my pajama

pants are sticking to my legs. I walk to my room, trying to ignore the fact that I'm in my bare feet. Most of the other girls are wearing flip-flops, but I didn't pack any. They were on the packing list, under THINGS TO BRING, I think, but I pretty much ignored that list. I thought they just meant flip-flops were in fashion here or something, not that we'd need them to prevent foot infections.

When I get to my room, Tia and Rachel are sitting on Crissa's bed. Tia has music playing from a small CD player, and she's dancing around the room, using a hairbrush as a microphone.

"We're alll in this toggeettther," she sings, spinning around. She thrusts the hairbrush in Crissa's face.

"Um, no thanks," Crissa says, pushing it away and turning back to the book that's in front of her. "Shut that off, I'm trying to study."

"First day of classes isn't until tomorrow," Rachel says. "So put your books away." She jumps on top of Crissa, who laughs and hits her in the head with a pillow.

I crawl under my sheets and try to ignore the fact that the three of them are ignoring me. I listen to them sing and talk about people I've never met. They don't even ask me to join in. I'm a horrible singer, but still. I love having private dance parties. In my room at home, I'd crank whatever was on the radio, and pretend I was giving a concert for millions of people. And sometimes when I go to the movies, when I'm walking down that lighted aisle to my seat, I pretend I'm a rock star, about to go onstage. I feel a tear well up in my eye, and I pull the blanket over my head to try and stop it from sliding down.

I must have fallen asleep, because the next thing I know, I open my eyes and see nothing except for the numbers on my clock letting me know it's 1:30. Great. I blink a little bit to get my eyes used to the darkness. Crissa's in her bed, her blankets moving up and down with her deep, slow breaths.

I close my eyes and try to get back to sleep, but it's no use. I tiptoe out of bed and over to my desk, where I boot up my computer and log on to my e-mail.

Two new e-mails. One that's spam from some knitting website, and the other one is from my dad. No e-mails from anyone from home, which isn't a surprise. I stare at the cursor for a long time, running it over the OPEN button on the e-mail. Open, don't open. Open, don't open. It's like a little merry-go-round in my head.

Finally, I click it.

DEAR SCARLETT,

I HOPE YOU ARE GETTING SETTLED INTO

BROOKLINE, AND ALL IS GOING WELL. I KNOW
YOU WILL DO FINE IN A NEW PLACE, AND I'M
GLAD YOU HAVE BEEN GIVEN THE OPPORTUNITY
FOR A FRESH START. EVEN SO, PLEASE KNOW
THAT I'M SORRY FOR MY PART IN ALL THIS.
I'M SURE YOUR IDEAL SITUATION DID NOT
INCLUDE BEING AT BOARDING SCHOOL.

I KNOW YOU'RE VERY ANGRY WITH ME RIGHT NOW,
AND YOU HAVE EVERY RIGHT TO BE. ALL I ASK
IS THAT YOU DO YOUR BEST TO TRY AND FORGIVE
ME, OR, AT THE VERY LEAST, ALLOW ME SOME
PART IN YOUR LIFE.

YOU ARE ALWAYS ON MY MIND AND IN MY
THOUGHTS.

LOVE,
DAD

I stare at the e-mail for a long time before deleting it and then crawling back into bed. But it's an even longer time before I finally fall asleep.

Chapter 2

So here's the deal with my dad. He's kind of a thief. And when I say kind of, what I really mean is, you know, that he is.

My dad's in a ton of trouble for stealing a bunch of money from his company, WebWorkz. They're this totally huge Internet provider, and my dad is their CEO. Or *was* their CEO, until he got fired for stealing money from them. It's this big story in the news, and if you turn on MSNBC or go to any of the news websites, they're talking about it constantly. And now that I'm at Brookline, I'm determined to keep it a secret. Which I *should* be able to do, since I have a different last name from my dad—I have my mom's name, Northon, since when I was born, my mom was going through a whole "I'm-an-independent-woman" phase, and since she kept her own name when she married my dad, she decided I should have it too.

It was not so easy to keep this all a secret at my old school. There, EVERYONE knew that my dad was Steve Haverhill, CEO of WebWorkz. I liked it. I milked it. I was kind of a celebrity. It was like being Bill Gates's daughter or something. But once the story broke that my dad had been embezzling a bunch of money to cover some bad investments he'd made, things started to change.

I wasn't Scarlett Northon, Steve Haverhill's daughter anymore. Now I was "Scarlett Northon, whose dad Steve Haverhill stole tons of money from WebWorkz and whose name is all over the news." Everyone at my school started talking about it. At first, it wasn't really that bad. Whispers in the halls. Weird little looks. But my best friend, Brianna, stuck by me, telling me to ignore everyone else. We'd huddle at our own table at lunch, eating sandwiches and reading magazines.

But Rockville is a pretty snotty town, and a lot of my friends' parents, who were friends with *my* parents, stopped inviting them to stuff. It was like they were afraid of catching a disease or something.

And then eventually *I* stopped getting invited places.

Brianna was still getting invited, though, and of course I'd insist that she should go wherever it was. I thought I was being a good friend, telling her she should hit up Shay Basile's birthday party instead of going to the mall with me like we planned, or that she should go to Chelsia Reade's vacation house instead of helping me with my science project. Eventually, Brianna drifted back over to my old group, and I was left alone at my cafeteria table.

Things hit a low point when one day, I overheard this girl Emma looking for her cola-flavored lip gloss after gym, and Brianna said, "I wonder if Scarlett took it—like father, like daughter," and they both laughed. I cried all afternoon, wiping the tears away with the sleeve of my new Michael Kors dress.

Add that to the fact that my parents started having all sorts of problems, and my dad moved into his own apartment while he waits to find out what's going to happen to him, and you can imagine that things weren't going so well for me. So when I suggested (read: begged) the idea of transferring schools for a fresh start in eighth grade, my mom agreed.

I never thought she'd go for it. I mean, come on—what mom just lets their kid transfer because they're having a hard time at school? Part of the deal, though, was that I go to Brookline. There are about three bazillion private schools around here, but my mom wanted to make sure I ended up at one that would allow me to focus on my studies, blah blah blah. If you ask me, I think she's just nervous that the same thing that happened to her would happen to me. And that is, she married her high school sweetheart, never went to college, never got a real job, and now might be losing everything.

With all this stuff running through my mind, I don't sleep too well on my first night at Brookline. By the time I do finally fall asleep, it's, like, four in the morning, and I sleep through my alarm when it goes off at seven. I only have half an hour to get ready for breakfast, since that's when the bell they ring to wake up all the students goes off. Half an hour! By the time I straighten my hair (which, by the way, I can't even do a very good job with, since I only have a limited amount of time, and because my hair is still half-wet from my shower last night—it looks like it's halfway poufed out and halfway not, and for some reason putting it in a ponytail makes it looks worse), Crissa and Rachel and Tia have already left for breakfast. They got so sick of waiting for me and so worried they were going to be late, that they ended up just going without me.

"Are you sure?" Tia asked, looking nervously between me and Crissa, who was tapping her sneakered foot on the ground and looking semimad.

"I'm sure," I said, not really being that sure at all.

I try to put my makeup on (lip gloss, some eye shadow, and lipstick) while I'm rushing out of the dorm and over to McGinty Hall where the dining hall is, but I drop the lipstick on the steps and end up crushing it with my foot. The bottom of my shoe turns into a slippery, light pink mess that I have to spend three minutes cleaning off. This is not a good way to start off the first day of classes. At least my uniform looks kind of cute—I dressed it up with some awesome Steve Maddens that go perfectly with the skirt, and I'm wearing patterned gray tights and a wide navy blue headband. It's so boarding school chic!

When I finally do get to the dining hall (I got semilost and accidentally ended up walking into some random girl's room—oops), I don't see Crissa, Tia, and Rachel anywhere. Finally I spot them at a table in the corner. I grab an apple off the side table, and a glass of juice off the counter. They don't even have coffee here! Usually on my way to school we stop at Starbucks and my mom gets me a caramel latte, but apparently today I won't even be having regular coffee. Figures, on the one day I need caffeine. I wonder if I can get a small coffeemaker for my room.

"Hey," I say, grabbing a chair from another table and scooting in next to Crissa.

"Is that all you're having?" Tia asks. "We don't have lunch until twelve." Her plate is piled high with waffles and sausage. Crissa's having toast with peanut butter and jelly, and Rachel has a huge bowl of cereal in front of her, along with some fruit salad.

"I know," I say. "I'm not much of a breakfast person. Usually I like my lattes, but they don't even have coffee here!" I roll my eyes.

"Coffee stunts your growth," Crissa says, frowning. Her forehead gets all squishy when she does that, with a big wrinkle. She's not going to be too happy about that when she's older.

"Well, I'm already five foot two." I take a bite of my apple. "So I don't need to grow any more. Besides, if my growth is stunted, I might get out of having to play basketball."

It's supposed to be a joke, but Crissa looks skeptical as she takes a bite of toast. All righty, then.

"So, anyway," Crissa's saying. "She totally thinks she's going to be first place this quarter, but it's definitely mine."

"What's she talking about?" I whisper to Rachel, who's sitting on the other side of me.

"First Quarter Math Award," Rachel says. "Every year the person with the highest math grade at the end of each quarter gets the Math Award." She must see the blank look on my face, because she goes on, "It's, like, a really big deal. Crissa's a shoo-in to win it." Figures they'd be talking about something having to do with schoolwork. Last night when they were gossiping about all the good stuff, they wanted nothing to do with me—now that I'm actually kind of sort of a part of the conversation, they're talking about a freakin' math award.

I wonder if they give out a last-place ribbon. I bet I would totally win that. But this, of course, is not the way a smart person acts. And today is the first day of Scarlett Northon, Smart Person. I pull my fake glasses out of my purse, slide them onto my nose, and look at Rachel seriously.

"So tell me about this math award," I say.

My first class is English, with Miss Cardanelli. I breathe a little sigh of relief. English is my best subject. I've always liked to read and write, and besides, a lot of stuff you talk about in English doesn't have any right answer. In math, science, and even social studies, you have to get the answer exactly right. In English, things are more open to interpretation. For example, last year I spent twenty minutes convincing my class that a poem everyone else thought was about death was actually about love, and by the end of the period, everyone totally believed it. I love stuff like that.

"Hello, class," Miss Cardanelli says, when we're all settled into our seats. She's wearing the best shoes. I wonder if it would be inappropriate for me to ask her where she got them. "And welcome to eighth-grade English."

The students shift in their seats. They all look very excited. I practice putting an excited-about-learning expression on my face. It's harder than it looks, especially when my eyes are so close to closing. I push my fake glasses further up on my nose.

"Now," Miss Cardanelli says, pulling a big white cardboard box onto her desk. "I have an exciting project for all of you this year." She pulls a bunch of envelopes out of the box, along with a stack of paper. "It's called stranger writing."

Um, okay. Sounds strange. (Must be why it's called "stranger writing"? Ha-ha.)

"Stranger writing?" a blond girl at the front of the room asks. "What is that?" She doesn't even raise her hand. Is this one of those places where students are allowed to just speak out in class? It *is* a charter school, after all. In one collective movement, everyone in the room pulls out a notebook and gets ready to take notes. Wow. I reach into my bag and pull out my navy blue speckled composition book, along with my blue feathery pen. I like my school supplies to match, just like my outfits. Ooh, *and* my school supplies totally match my outfit today. Bonus!

"Well, it's a name I came up with myself," Miss Cardanelli admits. She starts passing out the envelopes and papers to the class, weaving up and down the rows. "I saw a TV program over the summer about how we're more likely to share our deepest thoughts with someone who we've never met, rather than with our friends."

Hmm. I think I saw that too. It was on an episode of *Gossip Girl*.

"Oh, right," someone near the front of the room says. "It was a documentary on HBO."

Other people in the class nod. Jeez. Who had time to watch documentaries this summer? I spent most of it out by my pool. Oh, and we went on a totally fab vacay to Miami Beach, where I got to drink virgin daiquiris with little umbrellas at the hotel bar. Of course, my grandparents paid for me and my mom to go, since we're, you know, broke now. But I nod my head too, as if I watched it. No sense starting off on the wrong foot.

"Oh, I'm so glad some of you saw it," Miss Cardanelli says. I continue nodding my head, and even go so far as to add a knowing smile.

"Scarlett, what did you think of it?"

Um, that hanging out by the pool sounds way better? "Um, well," I say, "I thought it was very interesting." Interesting is always a good choice, because it can mean anything. It could mean you hated it or loved it, or it could mean you found it inspiring or you found it uninspiring, but either way, you thought it was *interesting*.

"What part exactly?" Miss Cardanelli is saying. And not to be mean, either. She looks like she genuinely wants to know what I thought about it.

"Um, the part about where people are more comfortable telling strangers things." I grope around in my brain desperately, trying to come up with something that will sound halfway intelligent without letting on that I never actually watched the show. "It's like how I am here at Brookline. I'm totally new so *everyone* is a stranger." I try to sort of whisper that last part ominously. That oughta work. No one's going to press me on being a new kid.

"Um," Miss Cardanelli looks confused, but she recovers quickly. "You're right about that, Scarlett."

"Maybe," I say, "someone could get the DVD of that show, and we could all watch it as a class and discuss."

"That's a good idea," Miss Cardanelli says, shooting me a smile. I settle back in my seat, feeling a little smug. This being smart stuff is a total piece of cake. I open up my notebook and write "Stranger Writing—letting strangers know your innermost secrets is easier than letting your friends know. Was documentary on HBO." Part of being smart is taking copious notes.

"So," Miss Cardanelli says. "We're going to be participating in a kind of experiment. We're going to be writing letters to an English class at Brookline Academy for Boys." A nervous rustling goes through the crowd. My ears perk up. Boys?

The blond girl at the front of the room raises her hand again. "But, Miss Cardanelli, what would we write about?" She looks nervous.

"Well, that's the thing," Miss Cardanelli says. She slides back into her desk chair. "You won't know who you're writing to, and they won't know who you are." She shrugs. "So you can tell them whatever you want."

I look around. The class looks sullen and definitely scared. I think they might be nervous that we'll be doing all this letter writing for nothing, but in my experience, if you're having any kind of contact with guys, it's never for nothing. I raise my hand.

"Yes, Scarlett?"

"At the end of this whole thing, will there be a mixer?"

"A mixer?" Her perfectly arched eyebrows knit together

in confusion. "Well, no, that's not really the point. The point is to work on our writing skills in a creative and new way." She reaches into her desk drawer and pulls out a Red Sox baseball hat. "What you'll do is reach into this hat and pull out a number," Miss Cardanelli says. "And that is who you'll be writing to. Their teacher at Brookline Academy for Boys, Mr. Lang, will be handing out the letters by number. No one will ever know who you are."

"Is this for extra credit?" Crissa's asking.

"No," Miss Cardanelli says. She sighs. She's weaving through the rows, letting everyone choose a slip of paper. "This is good practice for your writing skills, and you will receive a participation grade." The class still looks worried. Not me. I'm not. I'm never worried when it comes to boys. Not like I've had that much experience with them or anything. Although there was this boy at my old school, Adam, who everyone was positive liked me. Well, until that whole thing with my dad happened. Then he kind of started avoiding me. Not that it was that hard, since our contact had been limited to him walking me to math class after gym. But whatev. I push Adam out of my mind and focus on my new prospects. Guys at Brookline Academy for Boys. *Private school* boys. Who probably wear ties and button-ups. Who probably are smart and talk about fun, interesting things. I grab a piece of paper out of Miss Cardanelli's hat.

"Girls, there's no need to worry! You don't have to tell them your innermost secrets; you can tell them anything you'd like." Miss Cardanelli glances at the clock. "Now, for the next fifteen minutes or so, I'd like you to all write an intro letter. It doesn't have to be long or in-depth, and you don't have to reveal anything you're uncomfortable with."

She picks up a kitchen timer on her desk and sets it. "Go!"

Hmm. What to write, what to write.

I look at the slip of paper in my hand. It has a big "17" written on it in black Sharpie. All around me, girls are scribbling furiously. Wow. I guess when there's a grade involved, they get all into it and forget their fears.

Here's what I write:

Dear Number Seventeen,

Well, I guess I'm not allowed to tell you my name, but just so you know, seventeen is my favorite number. This is my first year at Brookline, and I actually do have a secret reason that I'm here, but I'm not going to tell you that. I don't care if you're a stranger or not. Although maybe if you're nice to me, I will eventually tell you. And then we'll be able to prove if this experiment actually works. Do you have any deep, hidden secrets?

Anyway, I'm not sure what else to write. Oh, except I totally got conned into joining the basketball team somehow. Do you play any sports? Do you have any basketball tips for me? Boys are all supposed to be good at that stuff, right?

Talk to you later.
Number Seventeen

I shove my paper into the envelope Miss Cardanelli gave us, seal it, and sit back in my chair. Everyone else is still working, so I reach into my bag and pull out the romance novel I'm in the middle of reading. This being smart thing is no sweat. Seriously, I don't even know what I was worrying about. This school is even easier than my old one. I mean, writing letters that the teacher isn't even going to read?

Piece of cake. I'm probably one of those complete geniuses who no one realizes is a genius until they get pushed, or decide they should work harder.

"Okay, class," Miss Cardanelli says when the timer goes off. "Pens down."

The class lets out a collective groan. I guess they can't all be fast writers like me. After everyone seals their envelopes, Miss Cardanelli tells us to open our books to page sixty-seven. "We're going to start the year with a refresher," she says. "Themes from *A Midsummer Night's Dream.*" Hmmm. Shakespeare? So much for being smart.

In math, I take a seat toward the back of the room, hoping this will ensure I don't get called on. If I'm in the back, I can sort of hide, right? I pick up my math book and pretend I'm engrossed in a chapter on fractions. God, it's hot in here. My uniform is way too long. I wonder if they have a sewing class here; it would be nice to maybe hem it up, put a cute little bow at the bottom, maybe some ribbon . . .

A strict-looking woman walks into the room and over to the whiteboard. She picks up a marker and slides it down the board. It makes a squeaking noise, like it's out of ink, and she shakes her head before throwing it back down on the tray in disgust. Yikes. Her hair's pulled back into a bun so tight it looks like her eyes are going to pop out of her face.

"Open your books to page two hundred forty-three," she says, popping the top off a new marker and writing MRS. WALKER on the board in big, angry-looking letters. The bell hasn't even rung yet, but somehow all of the students are here. That's ridiculous, starting class before the bell even rings. How will you know if you're late or not? How will— *RINNNNGG*. The bell goes off. Okay, then.

"Who can tell me the answer to problem number four?" Mrs. Walker asks. So much for a personal introduction.

I take a deep breath. Let's see, number four. This doesn't look too hard. I think it has to do with the quadratic formula. I pull a piece of paper out of my binder and copy down the problem with my pencil. I start to plug in the numbers, but before I'm even done, Crissa's hand shoots up.

"It's twenty-seven," she says before Mrs. Walker can even call on her. "The answer is twenty-seven."

"Right," Mrs. Walker says. "What about number seven?"

The class bends back down over their books, and I look around suspiciously for calculators. They *must* be using calculators. In high school you're allowed to use them; I've seen some of the older kids with graphing calculators. But graphing calculators were definitely not on the list of things to bring for school supplies, all it said was that we needed paper and pencils, a binder, and —

"Scarlett Northon!" Mrs. Walker yelps, and I jump. My pencil goes flying through the air and lands on the floor a few feet away from me.

"Yes?" I squeak. I slide my foot over the carpet and try to reach the pencil that's on the floor. Almost there. I try to slide it back to me with the bottom of my shoe, but it's too far away. It doesn't help that Mrs. Walker is looking at me with a very intense look.

"Number seven. What is the answer?"

The whole class turns to look at me. Actually, this isn't true. Only about half the class. Okay, so no one is really looking at me, but it FEELS like they are. The silence is starting to stretch. I rummage through my pencil case for a pen, so I can at least attempt to do the problem.

"Scarlett," Mrs. Walker says. She folds her arms over her massive chest. "We're waiting. If you don't know the answer, please say, 'I don't know.'"

I'm scribbling furiously. Nine times two divided by three is . . . seven — no, six . . . minus two, carry the one . . . "Seventeen and one-eighth!" I announce triumphantly. Take that, Mrs. Walker and all you classmates who seem to be staring at me!

Mrs. Walker fixes her cold stare at me, then turns to Tia. "Tia?" she asks.

"Nine and three quarters," Tia reports.

"Very good," Mrs. Walker says. "I see *most* of you are having no trouble with the quadratic formula, so I see no reason for a review." She walks over to the board. "Now open your notebooks and get ready to write down everything I say in EXCRUCIATING detail."

Excruciating detail. Yikes. I open my notebook hastily and then pick my pencil up off the floor. I feel tears starting to build behind my eyes, and I slide my fake glasses up and brush them away with the sleeve of my uniform. I will not let anyone see me cry. Besides, it was only one wrong answer. And it's the first day. No one's even going to remember it. I take a deep breath and turn back to the board so that I don't miss anything. But not before I catch Crissa looking at me and see the smirk that crosses her face before she turns back around to face the front.

Chapter 3

That night, all the eighth graders meet downstairs in the common room of the dorm for "get-to-know-you games." I am so not in the mood. The rest of my day was stressful at best. My classes are horrible. I'm behind in everything. (Although math is definitely the worst. When Mrs. Walker found out I didn't know how to convert fractions, she thought I was joking and almost laughed right in my face. When she realized I wasn't, her look turned to one of horror, and she told me we'd have to set up a time to talk, then sent me on my way with an extra review worksheet that no one else had to do.)

Then, at lunch, I had to ask some random girls if I could sit with them, and they had no interest in talking about anything that was remotely interesting. All they wanted to talk about was debate team. Snooze. I told them I was on the basketball team, but they totally weren't impressed. And speaking of basketball, I was so exhausted after my day of stress, that I fell asleep on my bed after school, sleeping through my first basketball practice of the season. I'm about to flunk out, and it's only the first day.

Also, why is no one here being nice to me? At my old school, people were at least a little bit nice to new people. Even if they just pretended to want to show them around the school to get out of class, they at least *tried*. So far, no one here has even attempted to talk to me. And from what I can tell, Crissa is the most popular girl here. How can this be? It's like this place is the opposite of any kind of stereotypes you've ever heard. Here you're popular for being smart and plain, where a good pair of Christian Louboutins and a Fendi belt get you nowhere. No one even seems too impressed by my Chanel glasses. Sigh.

"Welcome," Crissa says from the front of the room when I arrive in the common room. I guess she's in charge of the games. I slide down on the floor next to Tia. I'm wearing a cute pair of Seven jeans, a purple shirt that I found at this really cool flea market, and purple Skechers.

"Hey," I say to Tia. "Why is she in charge?"

"She's president of our class." Tia's still wearing her uniform. Most of the other girls are wearing pajama pants. Hmm. Does fitting in here mean I'm going to have to give up my whole wardrobe? That would be a shame. Although it does explain why the closets are so small.

"Already?" How can we have a president already? Shouldn't there be elections?

"She was president last year, so she gets to keep it until the new elections are held next month."

Oh. Right.

"It's time to play four truths and a lie!" Crissa exclaims from the front of the room. She's sitting on a high-backed chair, and since everyone else is sitting on the floor, she's looking down on us all. Fitting. Everyone groans.

"I know, I know," Crissa says. "It sucks since we all already know each other, but that's my job!" Everyone laughs, like she's said the funniest thing ever. Well, she does seem to have that whole slightly snotty, I'm-better-than-you routine down pat.

"Now, we'll start on this side of the room." She points to her right. Which is where I'm sitting. Lovely. "You all know how it works. You have to say five facts about yourself, four of them are true, and one of them is a lie. Then everyone has to decide which one is a lie, and then it's the next person's turn!"

Hmm. "How do you win?" I ask.

Crissa ignores me. "So! We'll start with you, Amber!"

I look next to me and see the blond girl from English this morning. True to form, she looks nervous. "Um, okay," she says. "Um, okay. Um . . . I have a brother, I don't like pink, I'm good at math, I have trouble falling asleep, and my favorite food is pizza."

Everyone in the room groans. "The lie is that you don't like pink," Tia says from the other side of me. "Bor-ing."

"I'm sorry," Amber says, shrugging. "I couldn't think of anything you don't already know."

Crissa rolls her eyes. "Scarlett," she says, "it's your turn."

"Okay," I say. "But how do you win?"

"You don't," she says. "It's a get-to-know-you game, not a competition." She looks like it's taking all her strength not to yell at me. It's not my fault I don't know how to play. Whatever happened to just going around the room and introducing yourself?

"Okay, let's see." I rack my brain for some truths and lies about me. I decide to take a page from Amber's book and keep it simple and boring. "I've never played basketball in my life, I'm an only child, I don't like chocolate, my favorite color is purple, and . . ." I try to come up with one more truth about myself.

But before I can, Crissa chimes in. ". . . and you came here for a really mysterious reason that you don't want anyone to know about?"

An awkward silence falls across the group. I can feel everyone's eyes on me, and the air suddenly feels thick, like a rubber band is squeezing the room. I look down at my hands. "Oh, sorry," Crissa says, forcing a laugh. "I was just joking around." She doesn't sound sorry. I think that's her pattern—she says a lot of things without really sounding them: happy to meet you, sorry, just joking around, etc.

"I think the lie is that you don't like chocolate," Amber pipes up. "No, no, wait. I think you said that to make us *think* that's the lie, but it isn't." She bites her lip and considers. "I think it's that purple isn't your fave color."

"You're right," I say, finding my voice and throwing Amber a grateful smile. "It's pink."

The rest of the game passes uneventfully, except for when Tia reveals that having her first kiss over the summer isn't a lie, and everyone has to stop and talk about it for, like, half an hour. It's actually kind of interesting. Apparently it was some boy who lives near her, and they'd been hanging out together all summer, and then finally before she left for school he decided to kiss her. She said it was a good kiss, not too slimy and not too dry.

When we get back to the room, I look at the mound of books on my desk. After my little nap this afternoon, I haven't done any of my homework. I open my assignment book and take a look at what I have to do. Hmm. Science reading, the math worksheet plus the regular assignment of ten problems, two social studies "mini-essays," and a bunch of comprehension questions and vocabulary words for English. They said they'd ease us into it slowly, and already I have more homework than I ever had at my old school.

"Don't worry," Crissa says, from where she's lounging on her bed. "You'll get used to it."

"Get used to what?" I ask, trying to pretend like I have no clue what she's talking about.

"All the work."

"I'm not *unused* to it," I say, which makes no sense. Crissa just smirks. She's reading her social studies and chewing on a gummy worm. My eyes narrow. Maybe I just need to break her down and eventually we will be BFF. That happens a lot in movies and books—people start out hating each other and then become the best of friends. Like in *Legally Blonde*. Plus Crissa is very smart and it wouldn't hurt to have her helping me with my homework. I work better in pairs, anyway. Brianna and I used to do our homework together almost every night. Well, until she, you know, stopped speaking to me.

Crissa's alarm clock goes off, and she reaches over and turns it off without looking.

"What was that for?" I ask.

"My hour of social studies is over," she says. "Rachel and Tia are coming over here to strategize soccer."

"Already?" Today's the first day of school. What can they possibly have to strategize about? Could this girl be any more anal?

"Well, I'm the captain." She grabs another gummy worm out of the bag on her bed. Of course she's the captain. I feel a tightness in my chest for a second, like I'm going to cry. Which is silly. I mean, just because everyone is going to be talking about soccer, and I'm going to be stuck on the basketball team is no reason to get upset. I'm sure there are loads of cool girls on the basketball team, who will be really nice to me, and we'll all have strategy sessions together in my room late at night while eating junk food and looking at magazines.

I sit down at my desk and open my science book. I'm about ten pages into reading about cell mitosis (bor-ing), when Tia and Rachel show up at our room.

"It's time to talk about kicking some boo-tay!" Tia says.

It's nine o'clock at night, and yet she's wearing a pair of navy blue shorts, a white T-shirt, and what appear to be shin guards and soccer cleats. Rachel follows behind her, wearing a similar outfit.

Crissa jumps off the bed and runs over to them. They jump into the air, high-five, and say something that sounds like "Hey rah rah something something Brookline Wildcats, gooo Wildcats rah sis something." It's all very confusing. I hope that's not, like, their cheer. They need a good choreographer.

"Wow," I say. "That's cool. What is it?"

Crissa looks shocked. "Oh," she says, swishing her hair over her shoulder. "I forgot you were here." She glances at Tia and Rachel. Um, where else would I be? This is my room. And I was just talking to her a few minutes ago. "That's our secret soccer club cheer. We're actually not supposed to do it in front of you unless you're on the team."

Great. First she brings out the fact that I don't want anyone knowing why I'm here, and now she's making me feel like an outsider in my own room.

"Oh," I say, hoping I sound nonchalant. "That's cool. Don't worry, I won't tell anyone."

I sit back down at my desk as the three of them pile onto Crissa's bed and start talking about their practice tomorrow.

My eyes feel all scratchy, and what with that making it hard to read, and the fact that the three amigas are talking and giggling like I'm not trying to study, I decide I need to go to the library. Which just goes to show how totally unbearable the situation is, since I have never once in my life decided to go to the library voluntarily.

I gather up all my stuff, shove it into my bag, throw my hair into a ponytail, and gloss my lips. Not that it matters. But lip gloss usually makes me feel better.

"I'm going to the library," I say to the room.

"See ya," Crissa says, holding up her hand in a half wave. Tia and Rachel don't even respond.

I head down the hallway toward the library. My eyes are still a little watery, and I reach up and angrily wipe them with the back of my hand. Whatever. Scarlett Northon does not roll over for a bunch of mean girls! Maybe this is karma for never trying to be friends with the dorky girls at my old school. But at least at my old school, even though I wasn't particularly nice to the girls who weren't in my crowd, they had friends. They had girls who they could talk to. All I want is to find one Fendi-wearing misfit here. Although I guess that isn't going to happen, since I haven't seen even one trace of Fendi since I've gotten here. I haven't even seen any Prada.

I contemplate this as I hit the bottom stair, feeling sorry

for myself. And then I hear a noise coming from under the stairs. It sounds kind of like a cross between a cry and a strangled moan, with a little bit of a sniffle thrown in. Hmm. Sounds like someone is crying and trying not to let anyone know. I used to do the same thing when I'd go to sleepovers and get homesick. Until one time in the fourth grade when Ella Markson's older sister caught me crying and woke up her mom, and my dad had to come and get me. And on the way home we decided that maybe it would be better if I didn't go to any more sleepovers for a while. But it was nice. My dad said it like we'd come up with the idea together, instead of just pointing out that I was obviously too scared to spend the night out by myself.

I creep around and under the stairs, and I see Amber sitting there, her uniform skirt sprawled out around her in a puddle.

"Amber?" I say. She buries her face back in her knees and doesn't move.

"I can see you," I say, sighing and crawling under the staircase with her. A film of dirt attaches itself to my jeans. Eww.

"What is it?" she asks, like I'm the one who's crying. Her face is still buried in her knees, and all I can see is a cloud of blond hair.

"Why are you crying?" I ask. "I mean, I've definitely felt like crying too, since I've been here, but you're not new."

Amber says something that sounds like "I'm hahschnick."

"You want a hot dog?" I try.

"No, I'm hoshnick."

"You need a hockey stick?"

"No!" she says, finally pulling her face up. Her cheeks are all smudged from her tears. "I'm homesick!"

"Oooh," I say, finally getting it. "You're homesick." That makes much more sense than her wanting a hockey stick. Although in this place, you never know.

"Yes," Amber says. She wipes her nose with the back of her hand. Eww. I reach into my bag, pull out a tissue, and hand it to her. She takes it and wipes her nose properly this time. "Are you?"

"Not really," I say. I miss my mom, of course. My dad, I could probably do without. But honestly I'm more worried about people here accepting me, and less about missing home. There's really nothing there for me to go back to. "I'm more concerned with people here liking me." It's out of my mouth before I realize this probably makes me sound totally shallow. "I mean . . . Wow, does that make me shallow?"

"No," she says. "It makes you *lucky*." Overhead, we can

hear the footsteps of students walking up and down the steps. She sniffs again. "I just miss my parents, you know? And my sister."

"Even after being here for so many years?"

"Yeah," she says. "It happens to me every year for the first few days. I get totally homesick." Sniff. "It's just hard with my dad being away."

"Where's your dad?"

"He's in the military, and he's stationed overseas." She's twisting her hands nervously in her lap. "I don't get to see him that much."

"That sucks." I can't really relate. Having my dad shipped overseas sounds fine to me. We sit there for a second, which is kind of awkward. I mean, I don't even know this girl, and she's crying in front of me. I'm not exactly sure what to say, so I decide to try my hand at speaking Brookline-ese. Or, you know, whatever it would be called if Brookline had their own language. I hold up my science book. "Want to go to the library and study?"

She looks surprised. "You're studying now?"

"Well, yeah," I say. "Why not?"

"Wow, you must really want to get ahead on everything," she says. She sounds impressed. "Usually people don't start pulling all-nighters until at least the second week."

All-nighters? Who said anything about an all-nighter? And more importantly, why would someone stay up all night *studying?* I love staying up all night, but only to watch late movies, or to do something I can't get away with during the day.

"Yeah, well," I say, hoping I sound smart, and not like I just spent the afternoon sleeping in my bed.

"Let me grab my stuff." She scrambles out from under the steps, and returns two minutes later carrying the most enormous bookbag I've ever seen. It's red and has wheels on the bottom — it looks kind of like the suitcase my dad takes when he goes on business trips.

"What are all those books?" I ask her, hoping I don't sound like I'm panicking.

"Supplementals," she says.

"Oh, right." What are supplementals? Never heard of 'em. I roll my eyes like I just forgot what supplementals were for a second. A slip of the mind, la la la. "I just haven't gotten mine yet."

She gives me a weird look. And that's when I see it. The tip of *Match Me if You Can* sticking out of her bag. "Hey!" I say. "You like romance books."

"Oh, not really." Her face flushes and she pushes the book back down, but it's too late.

"Amber," I say. "I know that flush. I've *had* that flush." I reach into her bag and pull the book out, running my hand along the spine. "I love this one!"

"Oh, me too!" she says. "Have you read the sequel?"

"Not yet."

She pulls another book out of her bag and hands it to me. "It's really good."

"Thanks." I put it in my bag for later. Not that I'm going to have too much time for pleasure reading with all this homework, not to mention my nap schedule. But still. "Hey, can I ask you a question?"

"Sure," she says.

"Is Crissa always so . . ." Hmm. What's the right word? Mean? Stuck-up? Conceited?

"Type A?" Amber tries carefully.

"Yes!" I say. "Type A." Type A is good. Very neutral-sounding.

"Well," she says, as we wheel through the dorm and out the door toward the library. "Not really. I mean, she's always been super driven and all that, but this year it's been worse." She leans in close to me, her bag bumping me in the knee, and lowers her voice. "She had a breakup."

"A breakup?" I try to keep the interest out of my voice

as we walk across campus to McGinty Hall, where the library is. The air's gotten a little cold, and I quicken my pace and keep my head down.

"Yeah." Amber's wheelie bag bumps over the pavement, the wheels screeching as it goes. "She was dating this guy James, from BAB, for like, all of last year. Their families are really good friends, she's known him since she was a little kid. And then over the summer, she breaks up with him. Supposedly she was heartbroken."

"BAB?" What's a BAB?

"Brookline Academy for Boys." Oh. Right.

"Why would she be upset about it if she broke up with him?"

"I dunno." Amber shrugs. "I guess it's just traumatic, you know? Plus their families are super close, and so she's always going to have to see him at, like, family parties and stuff."

"Her family has parties? I met her mom for a second, and she definitely didn't seem like the partying type." I try to picture Mrs. Bacon partying, and I giggle. Although my dad used to wear totally stuffy suits to work, looking all professional, and then sometimes, when my mom would be out for the night, he'd let me put on whatever music I wanted, and we'd dance around the kitchen while we made fajitas. It was the only thing my dad knew how to make. Thinking about those little dinner dance parties makes a lump come up in my throat, and I swallow around it.

"I was just using that as an example," Amber says. "I just meant she'd probably see him at random family events. And you're right about her mom, she's kind of a nightmare."

"How so?"

"She's wicked demanding. She used to come down here a lot last year, just show up unannounced and sit in on Crissa's classes and stuff, make sure she was doing okay."

"Jeez," I say. "And the school let her do that?"

"Yeah," Amber says. "Mrs. Bacon's on the board, they pretty much let her do whatever she wants."

"Wow," I say, pulling open the huge doors of the library. The warm air feels good on my face. "That sucks. So you think Crissa's still upset about the breakup?"

"Yeah," Amber says. "It was kind of this big deal, since she was the first one to have any kind of real boyfriend, you know?" We find a table in the back of the room and sit down. Amber starts pulling her books out of her bag, covering the table in a rainbow of pages. "Anyway, she's always been really driven, but now I think she's even more so. Like she's trying to prove to herself that she's okay and that she can accomplish anything she wants. You know, without a guy.

Plus I think her mom's putting even more pressure on her this year, since we start high school next year."

"Well, that's all well and good, women's power and all that, but maybe she should just find another boyfriend. Or at least stop taking it out on her roommate."

"I'm sure she'll be fine," she says. "She just needs to get used to you a little more. Her and her old roommate, Marissa? They were completely inseparable. Crissa was freaking out when she moved."

We spend the next two hours in the library, working on our homework. Well, I work on my homework. Amber works on reading ahead in our textbooks, writes in her journal, and works a lot out of her supplementals. Apparently "supplementals" are just what they sound like: books in addition to the books we already have. She also helps me with my math worksheet (which I guess is kind of like my own supplemental, since no one else has to do it, right?), which is really nice of her, especially since I'm not the fastest learner.

Recap of Amber helping me with my math worksheet:

Me: Oh, I get it! I just multiply this, and then . . .
(Writes down answer with mechanical pencil)
Amber: Right! Oh, except three times eight is twenty-four, not twenty-seven.

Me: Oh. Oopsies. (Erases answer) And now for this one . . .
(scratches in answer)

Amber: Well, no, you have to divide first.

Me: Right. (Erases. Hole appears in page) There we go!

Amber: See? Easy as pie.

Repeat process thirty times, creating thirty holes in paper and using up all erasers from mechanical pencils.

"Anyway," I say when we're finished. It's eleven o'clock, but I don't feel tired. Maybe it's the nap I took earlier, or maybe I'm just wired from the thrill of getting all my work done. "Thanks for coming to the library with me. And thank you so much for helping me with that."

"No problem," she says.

"I wish there was a way I could pay you back." And then I have an idea. "Hey, Amber," I say. "Do you know what Kiehl's are?"

Chapter 4

"Yes, Mom," I say *the next morning, resisting* the urge to roll my eyes. "I'm getting enough sleep." This, of course, is not true. Amber and I were up until two in the morning, down in the bathroom, doing makeovers! And the thing is, Amber actually *liked* getting made over! We did facials, and then I straightened and curled Amber's hair, and put lipstick on her. Then she did the same to me (she had some idea in her head that makeovers mean you do them to each other, and I didn't have the heart to tell her that usually you leave the making over to the person who's an expert.) She wasn't too good with the eyeliner. She kept poking me in the eye, but whatev. Also the makeup she used kind of made me look like a clown, but it didn't matter since it was so late. I just washed it off and went to sleep. Amber decided not to, and kept hers on. I tried to tell her it was a horrible idea, not washing off the makeup, since she was going to wake up all broken out, but she didn't listen. She said she'd never looked that good in her life, and she was going to keep it going as long as possible. For a second I was afraid she was going to have me snap a picture of her with my digital camera ("My dad loves getting pictures of me in the packages I send to him!"), but she didn't.

"What time did you go to bed last night?" my mom presses. I push the phone to my ear and study my reflection in the full-length mirror on our wall.

"Um, eleven o'clock?" I try.

"Scarlett!"

"What?"

"You know you need at least nine hours of sleep to function."

This is true. But since I took a nap yesterday, I suppose it all adds up. "I'll do better," I promise.

"Okay," she says. "What else is going on?"

I wonder if I should mention my trouble in math and the weirdness with my roommate to my mom. I don't want her to worry. I know it's normal for most moms to worry, but my mom is the worst. She worries about *everything*, even more so

 66

since all the stuff happened with my dad. "Not much," I say. I glance in the mirror and adjust the headband on my head. I actually woke up early today, even though I was up so late. Crissa was nowhere to be found when I got up. Probably getting a jump start on studying. Or making up new soccer cheers to annoy me with.

"How were your classes?"

"Fine." It's not really a lie. I'm sure they will be fine once I get used to the pace. That's what it says in all the brochures anyway. *"Although the transition to Brookline academics may be difficult for some, most girls will eventually adjust to the pace."* "Look," I say. "I have to go, or I'm going to be late for class." If my mom stays on the phone too long, she's going to start asking me a bunch of questions about my dad. I think of that e-mail sitting in my in-box, the one I deleted without answering, and I push it out of my head.

"Okay," my mom says. "I love you."

"Love you, too."

I grab my bag and head for Howser, the academic building where all my classes are held. I skipped breakfast this morning, so I'd have more time to get ready, and so I wouldn't have to deal with any potential "who do I sit with?" weirdness. I know Amber and I hung out last night, but that doesn't mean we're friends and I can go traipsing over to her breakfast table. Does it? I'm not sure. How many times *do* you have to hang with someone before you *are* friends? I haven't had to make new friends in a while. It's all horribly complicated.

The sun is bright, and the trees framing the sidewalk rustle in the early morning breeze as I walk to class. There's a little bit of a chill in the air, and I pull my sweater tighter around me and inhale the fresh air as I walk.

"Scarlett!" someone behind me yells.

I turn around to see Amber running toward me, her long legs tumbling over and over as she tries to catch up.

"Hey," I say.

"I looked for you at breakfast," she says, falling into step beside me. "But you weren't there." She shifts the handle of her huge red backpack to her other hand.

"Yeah," I say. "I was calling my mom so I skipped it." Yay! I have a friend! A friend who comes to find me in the mornings so we can walk to class together! I'm so thankful that at first I don't realize Amber is still wearing her makeup from last night. But on closer inspection, I see that Amber is not only wearing her makeup from last night, but it is very obvious that she slept in it as well. Her eye shadow is smudged, her lips are lined but the gloss has worn off, and her hair, which was curled to perfection just a few hours ago, now has the look of someone who's slept on their hairsprayed hair. Not a good look for anyone.

"Um, Amber," I say slowly. "Have you looked in a mirror this morning?"

"Yes," she says, smoothing down her skirt. "I'm a little nervous." She bites her lip, then leans in close to me. "What if people don't recognize me?" I must have a blank look on my face, because she goes on. "You know, because I look so different?"

"Right," I say. "Well, um, the thing is . . ."

"I mean, I know I'm not *gorgeous* or anything. But I definitely think I'm at least above average."

Oh, Lord. Amber thinks she's cute. Which, um, she is. Or was. Is. But since she's slept on her new look, she looks . . . a mess. There's only one way to handle this.

"Hey," I say. "Why don't we stop back at the dorm, and we'll give you a touch-up."

She glances at her watch. "I don't know," she says. "We only have a couple of minutes to get to English."

"We'll make it," I assure her, even though I'm not totally sure. But showing up to English a few minutes late is certainly better than showing up looking like a clown.

We head into the dorm while everyone is coming back out, their backpacks flying as they head over to Howser for classes. Going against the flow of traffic is not that easy. Ow. A girl steps on my foot, and I get bonked in the head with someone else's backpack.

Once we're in my room (a little banged up, but otherwise intact), I pull out my makeup kit, touch up her lips, her eyes, and then curl her hair around my big round brush. Not perfect, but it'll do.

"Better?" she asks, pursing her lips.

"Much."

We get to English thirty seconds late. "So nice of you girls to join us," Miss Cardanelli says. She doesn't seem mad, though, but more like she's scolding us because she has to.

"I'm sorry," I say, "It was my fault. I was on a phone call, and I didn't realize how late it was getting, and I made Amber late too."

"Just don't let it happen again," she says.

We head to our seats. The whole class is staring at us. Jeez. Haven't they ever seen someone be late before? At my old school, kids were late all the time. Sometimes they even (shock, gasp) skipped class. Then I realize they're not staring at me, they're staring at Amber. And then I realize they're not staring at Amber because she's late, but because of her makeover.

I hear someone next to me whisper, "Hey, Amber looks like Miley Cyrus!" And then Crissa whispers to Rachel,

"Why the heck would she do that to herself? She looks ridiculous." I smile as I slide into my seat and pull out my books. Crissa's jealous.

After class, everyone crowds around Amber, asking her about her new look. And when she tells them I'm responsible, girls keep coming up to me all day, asking where I learned how to make people over, and if I could do it to them. One girl even asked how much I charged! And someone else said I should do makeovers for magazines, like when they have before-and-afters. Then, in math, Mrs. Walker says my review sheet "looks good." Of course, she doesn't know it took me hours and that Amber had to explain everything to me a million times, but still.

I'm so excited about my day that I'm not even that upset when basketball practice rolls around. We're supposed to be meeting in "Gym A", wherever that is, at three o'clock. Why do the gyms need letters? And why do they need more than one gym for such a small school? I'm exhausted from being up so late, and the thought of running around and trying to get a ball into a hoop totally doesn't appeal to me, but hopefully it will be one of those things where there's, like, seventeen really good basketball players, and I just kind of blend into the woodwork.

"Hey," I say to Coach Crazy when I get there. She's standing in the middle of the gym, surrounded by five girls in basketball shorts. I guess the rest of the team isn't here yet.

"Who are you?" she asks, peering at me over her glasses.

"Um, I'm Scarlett Northon." She blinks at me. "I'm on the team." How can she not remember me? She practically begged me to join. She was like my own little basketball stalker.

"You weren't here yesterday," she barks. I see one of the girls behind her, a verrry tall girl with short brown hair, smirk and elbow the one next to her.

"Um, I know," I say. "I accidentally missed practice."

"Why?"

"I thought it started today for some reason." I shrug. "I'm new." No need to tell her I was cuddled up in my bed, taking a nice snooze.

Coach Crazy checks her clipboard. "Right, right," she says. "Here you are, Scarlett Northrop."

"Northon," I say.

"Why aren't you dressed, Miss Northop?"

"Um, I thought . . . Dressed in what?" I am dressed. Well, not for basketball. I'm wearing a pair of skinny-leg jeans and a red sweater. But I have my Nikes in my bag, and all I need is my basketball uniform, and I'll be good to go. Well, not good to go *exactly,* since I don't really know how to play basketball, but good to go in the sense that I'll be dressed to at least attempt to do *something.*

"Dressed in your practice clothes!" Coach Crazy yells. She throws her hands up in the air and her clipboard goes flying. The tall girl behind her picks it up and hands it back to her. Suck-up.

"I thought we had uniforms," I say. "You took my measurements." I'm beginning to think that Coach Crazy might actually really be crazy. As in, multiple personality disorder crazy. What happened to the sweet, pushy lady who signed me up? She's morphed into a psycho, one of those coaches who pushes their students so hard they end up on *Dateline* or some other news show, talking about how they ended up in the hospital from exhaustion and the pressures of middle school.

"We have uniforms for *games,* Northrop," she says. "And you're expected to have your own gym clothes. You think the school can just go around providing everyone with gym clothes? We're not made of money, you know." A giggle moves through the girls standing around her. I hope the rest of the team is a little nicer.

"Right," I say. There's an awkward pause. "So, um,

I guess I'll go back to my room and get changed into my gym clothes?"

"Good idea," she says. "And next time, don't be late. Everyone should be suited up and in the gym at three o'clock sharp."

"Right," I say. I run back across campus and up to my room. Crissa, Rachel, and Tia are there. Crissa's sitting on her bed, eating an apple, and Rachel is at Crissa's desk. Tia is sprawled across MY bed, a textbook open in front of her. Um, hello? Why is she on my bed? Better yet, why are they always in my room? Can't they hang out in Tia's or Rachel's rooms for once? They probably have smarter roommates who don't allow such imposing shenanigans.

"I thought you had basketball," Crissa says, not looking too pleased that I'm back.

"I do," I say. "But I wasn't dressed right. I didn't know you had to wear gym clothes to practice."

Tia snickers. Her feet are on my pillow. Gross. I have no idea where her feet have been. She may have been walking around outside with bare feet as far as I know. Or maybe she took her feet right out of her disgusting, sweaty soccer sneakers and put them right on my pillow.

"Could you not put your feet on my pillow, please?" I say sweetly. "I have a thing about it."

She sighs and moves her feet as if it's the hardest thing she's ever done. Jeez. What's with her? Crissa must have gotten her on the "I hate Scarlett" bandwagon. No time to think about that now. I run over to my dresser and pull open the top drawer. Let's see. What can I wear to basketball practice? The only workoutlike clothes I have are pajama pants. I have some shorts, but I don't think any of them would be good for running around in—they're not really athletic shorts.

I'm flinging things around my drawers, to no avail. Crap. Why didn't I think I would need gym clothes here? Probably because gym at my old school was a total joke. We'd spend most of the period waiting in line to take a serve at a tennis ball or something. Finally I spot an old Juicy tracksuit in the back of my drawer. Perfect! I pull it on and throw my hair into a ponytail, shove my feet into my new Nikes, then sprint back to the gym. When I get there, Coach Crazy barks, "Northon! Glad you could join us!"

"Me too, sir," I say, before I realize she's a "ma'am." No one seems to notice, which makes me think she gets called "sir" a lot more than one would think.

"You're just in time for suicides," she says.

Suicides? "Line up on the black line!" she barks.

The team lines up on the black line—well, the five girls

who were here before line up on the line. "Where's the rest of the team?" I ask.

"This *is* the team, Northon!" Coach Crazy says. Her hair is in a frizzy, gray cloud around her head, and she takes a swipe at her bangs, pushing them off of her forehead.

"This is the whole team?" There are only six, including me. How many people are on a basketball team, anyway? Does this mean I'm going to have to actually play?

"Yes," Coach says. "This is Andrea, Danielle, Rory, Taylor, and Nikki." I look at my teammates, who make no effort to tell me who is who. It doesn't really matter, since they all look the same—tall, tan, and tough. I can't tell any of them apart, and they don't say anything—except for the one standing next to me, the tallest one, who says, "There's only us; why do you think you even got on the team? We're desperate."

And then Coach blows the whistle, and the team runs up and touches the first line in the gym, then runs back to start. Then we run to the second line in the gym, then run back to start. We continue this for all six lines on the gym floor. Luckily, since I am the slowest one on the team, I don't have to worry about not knowing what suicides are. I can just figure out from following everyone else before me. By the time the suicides are over, I want to die.

"Hustle, Northrop!" Coach Crazy calls from the sidelines. "You're never going to make it moving like that!"

After suicides, we do a half-mile jog, push-ups, jumping jacks, and crunches, and then run shooting drills for an hour. The gym smells like a wet sock that's been left in the trunk of a car on a hot day, and every so often, one of my teammates will run by me and accidentally-on-purpose elbow me in the side.

"Good practice," the coach says when we're done. My hair is soaked with sweat, and my Juicy outfit is completely drenched. My legs feel like two pieces of wet spaghetti, and I can tell I'm going to have blisters tomorrow from running around in brand-new sneakers.

When I get back to my room, it's empty. Crissa must be at soccer practice. I fall back onto my bed, contemplating the hours of homework I have in front of me. *Maybe I'll just close my eyes for a second*, I think. What could happen? My mom even said I needed to start getting more rest. Then my eyes travel to my nightstand, where there are two pieces of mail waiting for me. Crissa must have put them there.

One's from the school, alerting us to the fall calendar — days off, school activities, etc. And the other one's from my dad. He must have sent it before I even got here. I run my fingers over the return address, which is his apartment that he's living in while he and my mom "figure things out." It's weird, seeing his familiar, black script with an address that isn't mine.

I wonder what my dad would think about me being on the basketball team. He was always trying to get me into sports. Every year, he'd convince me to watch part of this big basketball tournament on TV with him. It's called March Madness. We'd make sandwiches and eat chips, and I'd ask him crazy questions about basketball, and he'd laugh and pretend he couldn't believe I didn't know this stuff yet from watching it year after year. But I didn't really pay attention to the basketball stuff. It was just fun being with my dad. Of course, last year we couldn't do that, because there was tons of legal stuff going on, and my dad didn't really have the time to sit around watching hours of sporting events. Plus, you know, I was really mad at him.

There's a knock on my door, and I shove the letter into my bookbag to deal with later. Amber's at the door, and behind her is Rachel.

"Hey." Amber steps into the room. "We were waiting for you to get back from basketball."

"You were?" They were? Waiting for me to get back from basketball? Yay for friends waiting for me!

"Yeah," Amber says.

"Um, Crissa's not here," I tell Rachel.

"Yeah, I know," she says. "We wanted to know if you would make me over." She looks hopeful. Hmmm. Her hair has horrible split ends at the bottom. If she'd let me cut about an inch off, I could curl it and make sure it didn't lose its natural wave. And then maybe a plum eye shadow, and definitely some foundation . . . I must be lost in thought, because Amber cuts in quickly. "Of course, if you have homework to do or whatever, we understand. We know you just got home from practice."

I look over to my desk, where a pile of books are standing, about to fall over. I think about my assignment book, which is filled with things I have to do. I know I should do my homework, and especially study my math, but what if I tell them I don't want to hang out, and then they just forget about me? What if they're like, *Oh, Scarlett is so stuck-up, she doesn't want to hang out with us, so I guess we just won't be friends with her and ever ask her to hang out with us again.* And then what will become of me?

Plus, if I can get Rachel to warm up to me, maybe I can get on Crissa's good side as well.

"No, I'm not busy," I say. "I just need to take a shower, and then I'll work on you, okay?"

"Okay!" Rachel says, beaming. I shower quickly and return to my room to find the girls sitting on my bed, braiding each other's hair. At first I think it's cute, but then I realize they actually think braids might be a good look for them.

"Maybe, you know, as something to do at a sleepover," I say. "Or if you were going to do your whole head in a bunch of little braids, and put, like, beads or something on the bottom, like a Jamaican look, that would be cool. But other than that, no."

They immediately stop braiding. "Now," I say. "Rachel." I reach under my bed and pull out my plastic tub full of cosmetics. "How do you feel about a little haircut?"

Her hands fly to her head, and she grabs her hair. "Oh, I don't know, Scarlett," she says. "It's probably not a good idea."

"Bad experience?" I say. Everyone's had some sort of bad hair experience. When I was seven, I got a pixie cut so bad that random strangers used to think I was a boy.

"Well . . ." She glances at Amber nervously.

"I'm only going to take a little bit off, I swear," I say. "I'll make sure it's only this much." I hold my fingers about half an inch apart.

"Okay." Her face has turned pale.

I sit her down in my desk chair and look for something to wrap around her shoulders. Hmm. They use plastic capes in a hair salon, but where am I going to get one of those? I settle for a brown pashmina scarf I got last year at Calvin Klein.

"Have you ever cut hair before?" Amber wants to know. She's kneeling on my bed, getting ready to watch the whole procedure.

"Loads of times," I lie. In actuality, I've only ever cut Brianna's hair once and that wasn't even really a cut, since she just needed her bangs trimmed a little bit—they were getting in her eyes and driving her crazy. Oh, and one time when I was five I cut my cousin Ashley's hair up to her ears when I wasn't supposed to.

"Now," I say, studying the back of Rachel's head. "You must keep very still." I try to think of what my stylist, Vincent, does when he cuts my hair, but I'm drawing a blank. Usually I'm reading a magazine and/or talking on my cell phone, so I'm not really paying attention.

I grab some scissors out of the cup on Crissa's desk.

"Are those hair-cutting scissors?" Rachel asks doubtfully. She squirms under the pashmina.

"Well, no," I admit. "But it doesn't really matter. A good stylist is able to work with any kind of scissors."

They both nod, like they think I know what the heck I'm talking about.

I start to cut. The scarf isn't helping much, and big, fat chunks of Rachel's hair fall on the ground around my feet. I cut about an inch off, then step back to admire my handiwork.

"Hmm," Amber says. "Looks a little too short on that side."

She's right. I go back to cutting to even it out.

"Now it looks too short on *that* side," Amber announces.

I cut a little more. "I just have to make sure I clean this all up," I say, pushing some of the hair that's falling onto the floor into a pile with my foot. "Crissa will flip out if I make a mess."

"Yeah, she can be a neat freak," Rachel says. "I remember last year, her roommate Marissa left a huge pile of clothes on the floor before one of the dances we had. Crissa flipped out when she came home and found it."

"So she flipped out on Marissa, too," I say. "Good to know. The way she talks about her, you'd think she could do no wrong." By the time I'm done, the floor is a mess, and Rachel's hair is a little below her shoulders, when it used to be halfway down her back.

"Can I see?" she asks. "I want to see what it looks like."

"Er, no, not yet," I say. I grab my curling iron, and spend the next half an hour putting her hair into deep waves. Then I grab my makeup—a purple eyeliner, a cool plum lipstick and gloss, and of course some foundation to even out her complexion. Then I let her borrow my new purple sweater and tan cords.

Amber sits on my bed, leafing through magazines. I brought a huge plastic tub of them with me, and she's going through all my old issues, reading celeb gossip, and looking at the back-to-school fashions.

"Now," I say when I'm done with Rachel. I push a stray strand of her hair back into place. "Don't freak out when you look at it. Your hair, I mean. It's a *little* bit shorter than what we talked about, but—"

She heads toward the full-length mirror on the back of my door. She studies her reflection, and her jaw drops. For a moment, I think she's going to start yelling at me for cutting off all her hair. There's a silence, and then her face explodes into a huge smile.

"Oh my God, I love it!"

"You look just like a model!" Amber says, abandoning her magazine and clapping her hands excitedly.

"You are such a genius, Scarlett!"

Yay! We're all caught up in the moment, laughing and giggling, and I'm thinking, *Oh my God, I have friends and things are going to be okay after all.*

And then the door opens.

It's Crissa. She's wearing her soccer uniform, and, as an added bonus, a snooty expression. Mrs. Bacon is standing behind her. Her face looks like she just stepped in gum or something, all pinched up and disgusted.

"Oh," Crissa says, looking around the room. "I didn't know you had Amber over."

"Yeah," I say, "We were just, um . . ." I look around. There are magazines all over the floor, on both beds, and all over the desk. Makeup brushes are strewn about on my desk chair, and somehow a green eye shadow got stepped on and ground into the rug. On my comforter, a glittery bronzer has been spilled, creating sparkly brown streaks all over the fabric.

"We were just hanging out," I finish lamely.

"Oh," Crissa says, shrugging. "Cool." She wrinkles her nose and plops down on her bed.

"This room is a disaster area," Mrs. Bacon declares. She steps gingerly over a stack of magazines. "What is that on your comforter? Some sort of brown makeup?" She pulls her glasses out of her purse, slides them on, and moves in for a closer look. There's an uncomfortable silence. Even Crissa looks awkward. "You are never going to get that stain out."

No one says anything.

And then Crissa's eyes zero in on Rachel. "Rach!" she gasps. "You look gorge! Where are you going?"

"Nowhere," Rachel says, blushing through her plum blush. "Scarlett made me over."

A look of annoyance passes over Crissa's face. "What do you mean she made you over?"

"You know, she cut my hair and did my makeup." Her hands wander to her newly shorn locks, and she touches them nervously. But she doesn't sound as happy or excited as she did just a minute ago.

"Obviously." Crissa sniffs.

"So that's why you weren't at soccer practice?" Mrs. Bacon asks. She sounds like it's the most ridiculous reason she's ever heard.

"Well, no," Rachel says, looking uncomfortable. "I had a private tutoring session, and by the time I got out, there was only half an hour of practice left, so I figured it wouldn't be worth it to go."

"Mmm," Crissa's mom says. But it's one of those *Mmm, you just made a really big mistake* kind of "mmm"s. "Well, I should be going. I just wanted to check on Crissa's room, which has obviously fallen into disarray." I swallow hard and look at the floor. "I'll speak with you later, Crissa." With that, Mrs. Bacon flounces out without saying good-bye to any of us.

Nobody moves for a second, and then Crissa heads over to her closet and starts getting out her shower stuff.

There's an uncomfortable silence.

"Well," Rachel says, standing up. "Thanks for everything, Scarlett. Crissa, I'll, um, see you later in the library." She rushes out the door.

"I should go too," Amber says, looking at Crissa nervously. It's like the joy has been sucked out of the room, with some sort of special Crissa deflator. On her way out, Amber squeezes my arm. "Do you want to have dinner together?" she asks. "We could meet in the dining hall in like half an hour?"

"Sure," I say. Once she's out of the room, I start cleaning up the mess. I don't even care that I can feel Crissa's eyes on me as I throw tissues into the garbage and return the makeup and brushes back to their case. I'm too excited about my new friends and the fact that I have someone to eat dinner with. My stomach rumbles, and I realize I'm starving. Must be all that running up and down the basketball court.

"So," Crissa says as I'm sliding my bucket of magazines under the bed. "You're friends with Rachel now?"

"Well, not really friends," I say, trying to keep my voice light. "She just heard about Amber's makeover, and she wanted one too, so . . ." I throw a dirty tissue into our trash bucket. Hmm. It's getting pretty full. I didn't know we'd be using so many tissues to blend. My stomach rumbles again.

"Well, just so you know, you should be careful about how you pick your friends around here." Crissa lounges back on her bed, her hair falling in a pool around her pillow. She must notice that I'm giving her a death look, because she tries to backtrack. Well, halfway backtrack. "What I mean," she says, "is that we've all known each other for a really long time. So you shouldn't be disappointed if people don't accept you right away. Especially since nobody knows why you're here."

"Rude much?" I say.

"Look, I'm not trying to start anything," she says. Yeah, right. "But I just want to make sure that you don't automatically ruin your social future here. I mean, there must be some reason you left your old school. And I just wouldn't want to see you make that same mistake again."

I swallow hard. What is she, the friend police? Besides, it's not like she's been going out of her way to be nice to me and include me in all her popular-person activities. And from what I can tell, all those entail are going to soccer, studying, and walking around with a mean expression on her face. No thanks. "I think I'll be fine," I tell her. Then I finish cleaning up my side of the room, grab my bookbag off my chair, and head down to the dining hall to have dinner with Amber, pushing Crissa and her rude comments out of my mind.

The next morning, in English, we get letters back from our stranger-writing pen pals. Already? Who said e-mail was faster than the post office? Jeez.

For some reason, I have two letters. The first one says this:

Dear Number Seventeen:

It's nice to "meet" you. Well, kind of, anyway. My teacher, Mr. Lang, says this has something to do with "stranger writing." I guess he saw some documentary over the summer. Figures teachers would be watching documentaries on vacation. Anyway, I don't have that many secrets. Except for one time, when I borrowed my best friend, Tony's, favorite T-shirt, and I accidentally forgot to give it back. Actually,

I'm lying. That's the secret part. I really left it at my camp over the summer, but I told him that I just forgot to bring it to school.

I know a lot about basketball. I play all summer at my friend Ryan's house, although we cheat a little and lower the hoop so we can practice dunking. You probably can't dunk yet. Sorry you got conned into playing basketball. You should try to switch to soccer—that's what I play. It's pretty fun.

Hit me back.

Number Seventeen

How lame. He doesn't even have any big, juicy secrets. Well, that settles it. I'm definitely not telling him mine. Not that I would anyway. After the big debacle at my old school, no one is going to find out the real reason I'm here.

The second letter says this:

Number Seventeen,

Welcome to FOUR TRUTHS AND A LIE.
Over the next few weeks, I will be sending
you five declarative statements. Four of
these statements are true, and one is a lie.
It will be your job to figure out which is
which.

Statement Number One:

MISS CARDANELLI IS DATING MR.
LANG.

You have until Monday to figure it out. If
you choose not to participate in this game,
you are destined for darkness.

Good luck.

What is it with people here and this game? I look around
the room to see if this is some kind of joke. Like, part of the
documentary or something, where the teachers are trying to
see how bad they can freak the students out. But everyone

is reading their letters with interest, and no one else seems weirded out by them. Crissa's even got a little smile on her face as she reads hers. Figures. She's probably happy she has someone to flirt with, since she had such a bad breakup. She catches me looking at her, gives me a snotty look, and then folds her paper up carefully.

Of course I'd get the only psycho at Brookline Academy for Boys.

"You're lucky," Amber says later at lunch when I'm done filling her in about my crazy letter. "At least it's interesting. My pen pal sent me a very long letter about himself." She pulls it out of her book and clears her throat. "Listen to this. 'Dear Secret Pen Pal, My name is Stu. Actually that is not my real name, it is the nickname I am using for this exercise, since I have always wanted to be called Stuart. I am in the eighth grade at Brookline Academy for Boys. I like to play chess, and my dog's name is Muggles.'" She throws the paper down in disgust. "It goes on for three pages. I mean, hello. BOR-ING." She takes a bite of pudding from the little paper cup in front of her.

"At least it's not crazy," I say, picking up her letter. "He sounds nice."

"It's semicrazy," she says. "He ends it by saying I have

pretty handwriting. I think it was his idea of letter flirting or something."

"Amber! You have to give him a chance."

"Why?" she asks. "I don't see you giving your guy a chance."

"My guy doesn't want to flirt with me," I say. "He just wants to freak me out." Although it is kind of cute. And mysterious. Amber's right, I could have a pen pal who writes me super long boring letters (snooze.) And he seemed perfectly normal in the first letter. Maybe I should be thankful that my pen pal has a little spark to him.

"He wants to entertain you and be creative," Amber says. "Now, that is pretty cool."

"Do you think they're really dating?" I ask Amber. "Mr. Lang and Miss Cardanelli?"

"Well, did you ever stop to wonder how Miss Cardanelli got those letters to us so quick? Obviously they're meeting up somewhere to do the exchange."

"I wonder what he looks like," I say.

"Your pen pal?" Amber asks.

"No!" Although the thought did cross my mind. Not that it matters, since, you know, we're never going to meet. "Mr. Lang. I wonder if he and Miss Cardanelli are in love." True-to-life romance! I love it. "Maybe you could write a book about them." Amber looks skeptical. "Why not?" I ask. "You're on newspaper, and you're always scribbling in your journal."

"Writing in a journal is a lot different from writing a novel, Scarlett," she says. But before she can say anything else, a shadow falls across the table. I look up to see a very tall, very mean-looking girl standing over us. It takes me a second to realize it's the girl from basketball, the one who whispered to me before we started our suicides.

"Are you seriously going to eat that?" she asks, looking down at my plate. There's a blue keychain dangling from her backpack that says "Andrea" in swirly letters.

"Why?" I ask, horrified. "What's wrong with it?" Maybe she found out about some sort of weird thing going on in the kitchen. Or maybe there's mad cow disease going around here. I saw that on the news once, about how mad cow disease can live in your body for, like, twenty years.

"Um, it's red meat?" She gives me a look like I'm totally stupid.

"Ohhh," I say. "Are you a vegetarian?" I almost became a vegetarian once. After I learned about the mad cow disease. Maybe this Andrea from basketball is some kind of animal-rights activist. I practice looking interested and concerned.

"No," she says. "I just don't eat things that will make me slow during practice. But I guess it doesn't matter if you're going to be riding the pine the whole time."

She trounces off, her bookbag bouncing against her back.

"Wow," Amber says. "What was that about?"

"She's on my basketball team," I explain. "And I guess I'm supposed to be like, on a training diet or something. Although I'm not sure what riding the pine means."

"I think it means that you're not going to be playing at all," Amber reports.

"Great." I sigh and pull a french fry through my ketchup. I glance around to make sure Andrea's not lurking around somewhere, and then pop it into my mouth. "It's so weird, they all seem to be taking it so seriously, and I have no idea why. When I signed up, it seemed like they were desperate for players."

Amber frowns. "Basketball is the most competitive sport here. The team takes itself really seriously—they've been undefeated for, like, five years."

"So then why are they so desperate for members?"

"Because they're so tough—no one wants to join, because the girls that are already on the team are supergood and super cliquey. And the coach works them to death."

"Ugh." I drag another french fry through the ketchup. It's probably full of bad fats and things that are going to make me a horrible athlete. Am I going to have to become vegan or something? That definitely does not sound like fun.

"So what are you going to do?" Amber finally asks.

"I guess just try to do the best I can in practice. It's definitely too late to switch into something else."

"No." Amber holds up the letter. "I mean about this." She takes a closer look. "'You have until Monday to figure it out,'" she recites. "Well, that one's easy enough. Just ask Miss Cardanelli if she has a boyfriend."

"Oh, right," I say. "How could I do that? 'Hi, I got a strange letter and I need to know if you're with Mr. Lang, otherwise darkness will befall me or something.'"

"There are ways," Amber says. "I'm sure we can figure out something." She drains the last of her milk. "You wanna get out of here? We could go work on our math in the library."

"Sure," I say, but the wheels in my head are turning. Amber's right. I mean, asking Miss Cardanelli if she has a boyfriend wouldn't hurt anything, right? And it will give me something to keep my mind off of everything that's going on at home. Besides, I definitely don't want to come to some sort of bad end. I smile. It is kind of cute, what my pen pal's doing. That decided, I pick up my tray and follow Amber toward the trash can. As I do, one of my fries bounces off the tray and onto the floor. Yikes. I hope that's not some kind of sign.

Chapter 5

The next morning, I get called down to the headmistress's office before class. Getting called down to the headmistress's office is never good. Either something horrible has happened, or you're in deep, deep trouble. To make matters even worse, Crissa was the one who told me I had to go down there. Apparently she's a runner for the main office, which means she goes down one morning a week to run messages from the office to students. She showed up at our door this morning with a big grin on her face. She knocked on our door (yes, the door to her own room! She was totally doing that just to seem important) and said, "Rise and shine, Scarlett!"

I'd been up until two in the morning doing homework,

and even then I didn't get all of it finished. I was hoping I'd be able to work a little bit more on my math this morning, but it doesn't seem like I'm going to get a chance, now that I'm wanted in the office.

When I get there, the secretary, Jill, ushers me into the headmistress's office. The headmistress looks up from the papers she's going over, and gestures at me to take a seat at one of the chairs in front of her desk. Jill sets a glass of water down for me on the table next to my chair and then slips back out the door.

Wait a minute. Maybe I'm not in trouble at all. Maybe this is just one of those *I want to make sure you're doing okay in your new school, Scarlett, since I'm friends with your mother* kind of things. And then I'll be all, "Well, there's a little problem with Crissa Bacon" and Headmistress O'Neal will be all, "Well, she's probably threatened by your good looks and your obvious ability to adapt to any social situation." And then —

"Scarlett, I know this must be a very big transition for you, moving from your old school to an environment that you're not used to," Headmistress O'Neal is saying. It's kind of scary, her being behind that big desk like that. Very regal, with her gray suit and wire-rimmed spectacles and a big, important-looking painting hanging on the wall behind her. Some kind of abstract art.

"It is," I say, nodding and putting a sad look on my face. She's obviously setting it up to tell me what a fab job I'm doing here.

"And that's why I'm going to go easy on you," she says. Go easy on me? What is she talking about? She leans back in her swivel chair, removes her glasses, and sighs. "Scarlett, here at Brookline we keep the focus on academics. Do you know what I mean by that?"

"Not really," I say. I want to ask her if she thinks Crissa being so mean to me makes me able to really focus on my academics, but I realize now's not the time.

"What I mean is, we try to make sure the girls don't get distracted from their studies by frivolous things." She raises her eyebrows at me. They're perfectly plucked. I wonder if it would be inappropriate to ask her where she gets them done. My mom's coming to visit soon, and I could definitely use a trip to the salon.

"Right," I say, not sure what this has to do with me.

"Scarlett, we've had some reports of you . . ." she trails off. "Well, let me see." She picks up a sheet of paper sitting on the desk in front of her, and slides her glasses back onto her nose. "For example, it says here you shared your shampoo with someone the other day? In the shower?"

"Right," I say. "Someone on the other side of the shower

forgot their shampoo, and asked if they could borrow it, so I threw mine over." I'm in trouble for sharing my shampoo? No wonder people at this place aren't so friendly. They get in trouble for being nice.

"Which is great," she says. "Except your shampoo was something that cost at least sixty dollars a bottle."

"Well, I wouldn't go that far," I say. "Maybe like thirty. Although I'm not really sure; my mom buys it for me." I don't mention that maybe after this thing with my dad plays out, I might not be able to have that thirty-dollar shampoo anymore anyway. I'm sure she's aware of my financial situation.

"And," Headmistress O'Neal says, looking back down at her sheet. "It seems like you've also been giving some of the students here makeovers?"

"Yes," I say.

"Well, we've had a complaint from a student that these makeovers are very distracting. That students are coming in to class all made up, and causing quite a stir." A complaint from a student? She's got to be kidding me. Since when does a little eye shadow equal distraction? And then I remember the look on Crissa's face when she realized I'd made over Rachel. Of course she would complain about it. She doesn't want me having anything that's going to help me make friends.

"Well, I wouldn't call it a stir exactly, it's more like a little ripple of interest." I pull on the bottom of my uniform nervously. *Please don't ask me to stop, please don't ask me to stop, please don't —*

"Scarlett, I'm going to have to ask you to stop with the makeovers."

"But —"

"I'm sorry," she says. "But my decision's final."

In English, I write back to Number Seventeen.

Dear Number Seventeen,

I think you might be a little mental. (Of course, my judgment could be clouded by the fact that I just got in trouble for giving people makeovers here, and so I'm kind of in a "glass is half empty" kind of mood, but probably not.) However, my friend Amber (are we allowed to use names, even for our friends?) thinks that it's kind of cute and charming what you are doing. She's not really the best judge, since she got a very ridiculous letter from her pen pal, which was full of boringness. So I'm going to go along with your little game.

But like I said, I would still like the record to show that I think you are crazy. Which is fine. I'm used to being the sane one in my interpersonal relationships. I will mail you back on Monday with anything I've discovered about Miss Cardanelli and Mr. Lang.

In the meantime, would you like to tell me anything else about yourself? I'm surprised you don't have that many secrets.
I have lots.

Talk to you soon,
Number Seventeen

P.S. I think you should tell your friend the truth about his shirt.

Before basketball practice that day, I realize that Juicy tracksuits should definitely not be used for running. They get way too sweaty. They're more for airplane rides or, like, has-been celebrities who are going to be photographed by the paparazzi.

But I don't have anything else to wear. Amber's at newspaper, so I can't borrow anything from her, and I don't really feel comfortable enough with anyone else here to ask them to borrow their clothes. I'm rummaging through my drawer, hoping that something appropriate will appear, even though the chances of that are zero. It's like when you're hungry and there's no food in the house, but you keep staring into the refrigerator for, like, half an hour before you resign yourself to ordering Chinese.

Crissa's on her bed, talking on her cell to someone. Sounds like maybe to her old roommate, Marissa. They talk on the phone a lot. And text. Crissa has a special ringtone for her and everything. I weigh the options—interacting with Crissa, or getting in trouble with Coach Crazy.

"Um, Crissa?" I ask sweetly. "Is there any way you'd let me borrow some of your clothes?"

"My clothes?" she asks, throwing her head back and laughing. "Why would you want to borrow something of mine?"

"I need them for basketball," I say.

She rolls her eyes. "Second drawer." She turns immediately back to her conversation, something about how she hopes next year she gets to pick her own roommate.

I open her drawer, which is filled with brightly colored T-shirts and shorts, all folded neatly and sorted by colors. Hmm. I select a pink T-shirt and a pair of black cotton shorts. I push them into my bag, and sprint over to the gym. Everyone is dressed and ready. Except for me. "Nice of you to join us, Northon," Coach Crazy says. "Extra suicides since you're late." Great.

"It's just something I overheard Miss Cardanelli saying today," Amber says. We're in the newspaper office after dinner. I'm doing my math homework, and Amber's working on a story about school lunches for the paper. Why are there always stories in the paper about school lunches? There should totally be a gossip column. But when I brought this idea up to Amber, she said they tried that once, but Crissa's mom and the board shut it down because it distracted from the academics. Figures.

"What was she saying?" I ask, wondering if it has anything to do with my English grade. We haven't had any real English assignments, but maybe I'm getting behind anyway. I wouldn't be surprised.

"Well, this morning I was in here before school, because

we had this story I wanted to finish up, and Miss Cardanelli was there, because she's the advisor, right?"

"Right." I definitely should have joined newspaper. Much better. Sitting in a nice office at a nice computer all day, instead of spending your afternoons running around practically killing yourself. I feel like my legs are going to fall off. After Coach made me run extra suicides, I had to do the mile run with everyone else, and then shooting drills until I felt like my arms were two strands of spaghetti. To add insult to injury, Coach kept saying, "Northon, keep your arms up!" and "Northon, that's not the way to hustle!" And "Northon, you're not in elementary school anymore!" Every time she'd shout something, I'd get more and more nervous, and I'd drop the ball. And the girl who yelled at me at lunch the other day, Andrea Rice, kept slamming into me when I'd go and try to take a shot, and then Rory or Nikki would jump in the air and yell, "THAT'S DEFENSE, BABY!" I don't understand. Defense against your own team? Why do we play *against* each other in practice? That makes no sense whatsoever.

"So I'm sitting here at the computer," Amber says, "and Miss Cardanelli gets a call on her cell phone, and she goes, 'Excuse me, Amber, I have to take this' and I said no problem, even though teachers are totally not supposed to have cell phones in front of the students, much less be taking calls on them during school hours."

"They're not?"

"No."

"How do you know?"

"Because it's in the Brookline Academy Handbook, Rules of Teacher Conduct, Article six." She looks at me as if it's totally obvious. I have a vague memory of a blue paper-bound book that was mailed to me a few weeks before school started. I think I threw it in my desk at home, which is where it is now.

"Oh, right," I say. "Article seven, totally."

"Six," she says.

"What?"

"It's article six, not seven."

"Right, article six, I must have been confused for a minute."

"Right," she says, giving me a weird look. "Anyway, so she says, 'I have to take this' and then she goes out in the hall, which really was kind of silly since the door was open and I could hear everything she was saying."

"Who gets phone calls at seven in the morning?" I say. "Although I guess teachers do, since they have to be up so early. And since they're older and everything. Older people are always getting up early when they don't have to. Sometimes my mom meets her friends at—"

"Scarlett!"

"Oh, right, sorry, go ahead."

But we're interrupted by two girls who are approaching our table. Until now they've been in the back of the room, working on something Amber said was the layout. "Are you Scarlett Northon?" one of them asks.

"Who wants to know?" Amber asks, all toughlike. Which is kind of funny, since Amber's probably the smallest girl in our class, and because since these girls are on newspaper with her, she probably already knows them. It's cute that she's sticking up for me, though. I throw her a grateful smile, even though saying "Who wants to know?" is pretty much like admitting you are the person they're looking for; otherwise, why wouldn't you just say "no"?

"We want makeovers," the girls say.

"Sorry," I say, "but I'm not doing them anymore."

The girls walk sadly back to their station. One of them has the craziest curly hair, and I'll bet with a straightening iron, it would have looked fab. And some smoky blue eye shadow on the other one would have really made her eyes look amazing.

"What do you mean, you're not doing them anymore?" Amber asks.

"I got in trouble this morning," I say. "Because Headmistress O'Neal thinks I'm distracting the students by giving them something that focuses on their looks."

"That's ridiculous," Amber says.

"I know. So, anyway, back to your story. So Miss Cardanelli goes out into the hall with her phone."

"Oh, right. So she goes out into the hall with her phone, but I can obviously hear everything she's saying."

"Obviously."

"And she says to whoever she's talking to, 'Well, I have to chaperone the off-academy this weekend, so maybe you could meet up with me.'" Amber raises her eyebrows, as if this should impress me somehow.

"What's the off-academy?" I ask, my stomach dropping. It probably has to do with school. Or grades. That sucks. I was really looking forward to this weekend. Sleeping in. Lounging in bed. Maybe doing some online shopping . . .

"Didn't someone tell you about the off-academy?" Amber asks, looking shocked.

"No." I guess you'd probably learn things like that from your roommate, and since mine hates me, I don't know any of the lingo around here.

"Sometimes on the weekend there's an off-academy," Amber says. "It's basically like a field trip, to a different location every time. Like, sometimes we get to go out to lunch, sometimes we walk around at the mall, that kind of thing."

"Oh," I say. "Sounds fun." I'm not sure what Miss Cardanelli and her phone call have to do with all this.

"So Miss Cardanelli is chaperoning tomorrow," she says. "And she was on the phone, telling someone she'd meet up with them."

"Okay . . ."

"And she was saying it all flirtylike, like it was a guy on the other end."

"So you think she's meeting up with Mr. Lang?"

"I think she's meeting up with someone, and it's definitely a boyfriend-type person. I can't imagine she'd talk to her girlfriends like that." Amber's hands are flying over the keyboard. I have no idea how she can keep her mind on school lunches enough to type about them while she's talking to me at the same time. Very talented, that Amber.

"But we don't even know what Mr. Lang looks like," I say. "Although teachers all have a certain look about them. I think they wear button-downs a lot."

Amber giggles.

"I think we should follow her tomorrow," I say. "And just see what happens. Are you in?"

"I'm in."

Chapter 6

The next morning, Saturday, I meet Amber outside the academic building so we can wait for the bus that's going to take us to the mall. It seems like most of the school is going on the off-academy, which is surprising. I figured most of the girls here wouldn't be interested in shopping. When I ask Amber about this, she says, "But they have the Discovery Store at the mall, along with that huge office supply place. And the pet store takes up most of the second floor." Right.

"So what's the plan?" Amber asks once we're settled into our seats on the bus. Why do buses always smell like old gym socks and vomit? One great thing about boarding school is not having to ride the bus. I try not to breathe through my nose.

"What do you mean?" I ask. I'm having trouble focusing on any kind of plan. It's only ten o'clock, which is quite a ridiculous hour to be awake on a Saturday, especially since I'm still getting used to going without coffee. At least I look adorable. I'm wearing a gray Michael Kors dress with a drop waist and three-quarter length sleeves, gray tights, a long silver necklace, and chunky black shoes. My hair is straightened and my lips are glossed. My uniform is currently in a ball on my bedroom floor, and I don't plan on picking it up until Monday.

"I mean, how are we going to figure out what the deal is with Miss Cardanelli?" Amber asks. "We can't just follow her around, can we?"

"Why not?"

"Well, won't that look a little suspicious? Won't she be like, 'Why are Amber and Scarlett following me around?'"

"Maybe," I say. "But we'll keep our distance." I lean my head back against the seat as the bus goes hurtling down the highway. I wonder if I could just take a little nap. Closing my eyes would be nice. A little catnap, so that I'll be awake and alert for our big excursion. Ha. It's funny that a trip to the mall has suddenly become a big excursion.

"Well," Amber's saying. She lowers her voice and shifts on the seat next to me. "I *did* bring something to help us."

I reluctantly force my eyes open. Amber reaches into her backpack and pulls out the corner of something black and shiny. She leans in even closer. "They're disguises."

Great. What sort of disguises could she possibly have just lying around? There's no way I'm wearing those ridiculous plastic glasses with the plastic nose attached.

When the bus pulls up in front of the Evergreen Mall, I feel my spirits lift. I love the mall. Last year I spent practically every weekend at the mall—walking around, trying on clothes, getting free makeovers at the makeup counters, and hanging out with my friends. And buying anything I wanted. Of course, that was before the story about my dad broke. Then I remember that I never opened the letter my dad sent me, and my stomach starts to feel like a rubber band is wrapping around it.

"You okay?" Amber asks, squeezing my hand.

"Yeah, fine," I say, forcing a smile.

"Attention, ladies," Miss Cardanelli says from the front of our group. We all huddle up in the lobby. "You know the rules, but just in case, I'm going to go over them again. You must stay with a buddy at all times. You must make sure you meet in the food court in two and a half hours. Two and a half hours. That means at one o'clock *sharp*. We will all be eating together, and then going to see a movie. If you need anything, please come and find me—I will be having coffee and reading a book at the bistro near the food court. And if there's an emergency, please alert one of the mall staff."

"She looks kind of dressed up for an off-academy," Amber says, her eyebrows shooting up. We watch as Miss Cardanelli waits for all the girls to start filing into the mall. She's wearing a pink flippy skirt and a light pink sweater, and her hair is curled. A long gold necklace is tied around her neck, and she's wearing white high-heeled shoes.

"She looks cute," I say. "Although she shouldn't be wearing those shoes after Labor Day."

"Why not?" Amber frowns.

"Because they're white." Amber looks confused. "Never mind," I say. "So what should we do?"

"I guess wait until she heads to the bistro," Amber says. "And then we can follow her and see who she's meeting."

"Okay," I say. We stand in the lobby and wait as Miss Cardanelli talks to Andrea Rice, the girl from my basketball team, about something having to do with an assignment. Finally, Andrea leaves and it's just the three of us standing in the lobby. Awwwwkwarrd.

"Quick," I say, "pretend you're looking at the newspapers." There's a rack of free newspapers and booklets against the wall, and Amber and I pretend we're paging through them. "Oh, look!" I say excitedly. "This is a whole book about finding an apartment!"

Amber frowns, and I elbow her in the side. "Oh, right!" she says brightly. "That's good since you were, uh, looking for your first apartment?" She says it like a question.

"Can I help you girls with anything?" Miss Cardanelli asks. She walks over to where we're standing.

"Oh, no thanks," I say brightly. "We just figured we'd look through these newspapers before we head into the mall." I pick up one that says *AutoTrader* and start thumbing through it. Hmm. It's actually never too early to start thinking about your first car. Although I'm not sure I want to get mine out of the *AutoTrader*; these seem a little junky. I think I'd do better with a newer car, something in red maybe, with a top that goes down.

"Now, those are called tabloids," Miss Cardanelli is saying. "Because of the way they open." She demonstrates the way the newspaper opens like a book, instead of like a normal paper. This is why teachers shouldn't be allowed out in public. They always want to teach you something. To my surprise, Amber starts encouraging her.

"I'd think it'd be easy to start work at a tabloid right out of school," she says. "Since a lot of these come out every day, and they seem like smaller publications."

"You're right," Miss Cardanelli agrees. "But why not shoot for the stars, Amber? You could get a job at the *Boston Globe*, or the *New York Post*!"

"Fab!" I say. "That's so great!" I'm hoping this will put an end to the convo, but Miss Cardanelli mistakes my enthusiastic response for interest.

"Scarlett, I had no idea you were so interested in journalism," she says.

"Oh, yeah, I love journalism," I say.

"Well, I had a feeling you were a writer, since you seem to be really enjoying writing to your secret pen pal." She smiles a wide smile. I wonder if she'd be smiling like that if she knew my secret pen pal was interested in her personal, private business. "And, of course, we know Amber here is a writer, the way she's always scribbling in that notebook of hers." Amber blushes.

"Well, I like to read," I say uncertainly.

"So you want to be a novelist!" she says, clapping her hands together. "That's wonderful! Maybe we should do a lesson on publishing." She pulls a small notebook out of her purse and starts writing down notes to herself and muttering about the lesson. Amber and I glance at each other, and just stand there awkwardly.

"So!" Miss Cardanelli says, capping her pen and giving us a big smile. "You girls better run along now!"

"Oh, right," I say. "Well, I think we'll just stay here a little longer and look at the newspapers. I mean, uh, tabloids."

Miss Cardanelli smiles at my use of the new word, and Amber picks up the *AutoTrader* as if to emphasize my point.

"Girls, I think it's wonderful that you're so interested in this stuff, but I think it would be good for you to have a little fun. That's what an off-academy is for! Now come on!"

"But—" I try to protest, but she has a hand on both of our backs, and is steering us into the mall.

"No buts," she says. "You can grab some of those papers on the way out."

Great. I look at Amber helplessly. She just shrugs. Finally, we're able to duck into a store while Miss Cardanelli goes on her way, presumably up to the bistro.

"Now what?" Amber asks, pulling on her hair.

"Now I guess we have to wait a bit," I say. "It would have been better if we could have just followed her right off the bat, taken a look to see if she was with Mr. Lang, and then spent the rest of the time shopping. But we can't do that now; she's already seen us and she knows we're acting weird. We're going to have to wait a little bit, and then follow her up there."

"Hopefully she'll still be there," Amber says.

"I think she will," I say. "I mean, she said if we needed anything that's where she'll be."

"Well, then hopefully *he'll* still be there," Amber says.

I sigh. "We might as well look around for a little while," I say.

"Good idea," Amber says.

We spend the next half an hour trying on clothes in Bebe. I buy a cute pink sweater, and Amber gets a wide navy blue belt she can use to dress up her uniform.

"Okay," I say as we head out of the store, swinging our bags happily. "Now, we're going to have to be very careful when we head to the bistro. We're going to have to spot Miss Cardanelli without her spotting us."

"You know what we need," Amber says, her eyes glistening. Uh-oh.

"What?" I ask warily.

"The disguises." She leads me over to a bench and pulls two wigs out of her bag. One is black and shiny, the other is red and curly. She also has two sweatshirts, one that says DUKE UNIVERSITY and the other that says I DO IT BECAUSE I CAN.

"Those are disguises?" I ask.

"Well, they're not billed as disguises, no," she says. "The wigs are left over from some costumes the drama club used last year."

"And the sweatshirts?"

"I got them from the lost and found." I raise my eyebrows at her. "Don't worry, I washed them first," she adds quickly.

That was the least of my worries, but whatever.

"I don't know," I say slowly. "What if she sees us wearing wigs and weird sweatshirts?"

"She won't," she says. "She's not even going to be looking for us, and she's not going to recognize the hair." She holds up the wigs and shakes them.

"Fine," I say, sighing. So much for looking cute in my Michael Kors dress. Amber pulls the Duke sweatshirt over her head, so I have no choice but to put on the one that says I DO IT BECAUSE I CAN.

"Which wig do you want?" she asks. I opt for the black one, since the other one kind of looks like something a clown would wear. Amber got the better sweatshirt, so I figure it's only fair. Plus, hello, red hair would certainly not go with my complexion.

We head up to the second floor, hoping it will be one of those places that has seating right outside. But it isn't. There's a hostess at the door. After a whispered convo, Amber and I decide we'll try to just head into the restaurant, pretending that we already have a table in there, or that we're meeting someone. We're hoping we'll just be able to look around, see if Miss Cardanelli is with a guy, and then hightail it out of there. But the hostess, who's not even that much older than us, decides to get all snippy. (Plus she has horrible nails, done in this totally horrendous pink color that is not appropriate for fall at all, but that's a whole other story.)

"Excuse me, girls," she says. "Can I help you?"

"No thanks," I say, flipping my newly acquired long black hair over my shoulder breezily. "We're fine."

"Do you need a table?" she asks.

"Oh, no," Amber says. "We're meeting our parents here."

"Your parents?" She frowns and bites her lip, done in another shade of pink (also not appropriate for fall. Actually, not appropriate for anything.).

"Yup," I say. "Our parents."

"We're sisters," Amber explains, giving her a smile.

"Don't we look alike?" I ask, hoping to confuse her. It's a tactic I use on my mom sometimes when I want something and I don't think she's going to give it to me. I just talk and talk until she's so confused she doesn't have any idea what I'm talking about, and then she gives me what I want.

"Not really," the hostess says, looking bored. "Although you're wearing wigs, so I can't really tell." She peers at us. "You might have the same hair."

Amber and I look at each other in shock. She can tell we're wearing wigs? Although I guess it is kind of obvious. Amber's hair is sticking out from hers, and up close you can definitely tell it's a wig, since the fake hair looks kind of like thread. I don't expect mine looks any better.

"Well, we're in a production of *Romeo and Juliet*," I say. "We've just come from the theater, and we're meeting our parents for an after-show lunch."

Amber nods.

"Well, let me show you in, then," the hostess says. "You know, to your parents' table."

We follow her morosely into the restaurant.

"Hmm," I say. "Well, there they are." I see a couple sitting over near the window. "So we'll be going now."

"I'll walk you over," the hostess says. What is with her? She starts marching over to the couple, and Amber and I shoot each other a look of panic. There's no way we're going to be able to sit down with some random couple. I mean, I'm good at getting my way, but even *I* wouldn't be able to convince someone I'm their daughter when I'm not.

"Uh, actually," I say, trying to look confused. "That's not them." The hostess raises her eyebrows.

"Yeah," Amber says. "That's definitely not them."

She elbows me in the side, hard, and I follow her line

of sight. There's Miss Cardanelli, over in the corner, sitting by herself. She's reading a book and sipping an iced tea.

"Then where are they?" the hostess asks.

"Where are who?" I'm having trouble keeping up with this conversation. There's too much going on, what with the wigs and the fake parents and worrying about getting caught.

"Your parents!" the hostess says. She seems like she's about five seconds away from calling security on us.

"They must not be here yet," Amber says.

"Yeah, they must not be here yet," I say. "So we'll just have a table for two."

You can tell the hostess doesn't really believe us, but what is she supposed to do? She doesn't really have a choice. "Right this way."

She sets us up in a corner booth, the perfect spot to spy on Miss Cardanelli. Amber starts to get a little too cocky. "Now, when our parents come," she's saying, "make sure you send them right over here so they don't have to find us."

"Of course," the hostess says. She sets two menus down on the table in front of us. Once she's out of the way, I sigh in relief.

"That was close," I say. "We almost made a scene, and

if we'd made a scene, Miss Cardanelli definitely would have noticed."

"We should come up with a story beforehand, so that if we do get caught, we'll have something to say."

"There's no way we could come up with anything believable as to why we're in this bistro wearing wigs and stolen sweatshirts."

"Not stolen," Amber says, looking offended. "The rules state that if something is left in the lost and found for over thirty days, it's fair game. And these sweatshirts were there since last year."

"You know what I mean," I say. I look out of the corner of my eye to where Miss Cardanelli is sitting. "She's by herself," I say to Amber. "What should we do?"

"Hello!" a voice says, and I jump. A waitress is at our table. Great. "Can I get you girls a drink?"

"Um," I glance down at the menu. "A 7UP please."

"Shirley Temple for me," Amber says. I raise my eyebrows at her. "What?" she says. "It's a special occasion, what with us being in a play and all."

I giggle and the waitress leaves to get the drinks.

Amber and I look over at Miss Cardanelli.

"Well, he might just not be here yet," Amber says. "So I say we hang out and just wait and see if he shows up."

"Good idea," I say. "It will be fun. We'll just sit here and order some drinks and talk."

An hour later, it's not so fun. We hardly have any money, since we spent most of it at Bebe, so we've switched from ordering sodas to ordering waters, which is making the waitress slightly annoyed. Also, she keeps asking us if we'd like to use the phone to call our parents, when, hello, we don't need to, because there *are* no parents. So we keep saying, "Oh, no, they're always late, ha-ha" which, you know, isn't true. And I think she knows it.

"Maybe we should just go," I say.

"Are you crazy?" Amber asks. "We've waited here this long."

"True," I say. And at that moment, a brown-haired man walks into the bistro and sits down next to Miss Cardanelli.

"Yes," I say, pumping my fist.

"How do we know that's him?" Amber asks, frowning.

"Good point," I say. And then I see his jacket, which has BROOKLINE ACADEMY FOR BOYS embossed on the back. Bingo.

We have a little while until we have to meet up with everyone else in the food court, so Amber I decide to split up for a few minutes. Amber heads off to look in the Discovery Store, and I head to the bookstore.

When I get in the store, I take a few laps around, and then spot the romance section, all the way in the back. Buying books from the romance section is tricky. You have to be careful not to draw attention to yourself. One time I was in a Borders, and an older, grandma-type woman complained to the staff that I was too young to be in this section. She said the book covers and subject matter weren't appropriate for someone my age.

Thankfully, my dad stuck up for me. He told the Borders employee and the evil grandma type that he trusted me to choose my own reading material. My dad and I used to go to the bookstore almost every Sunday. He didn't care that I read romance books. I'd load up my arms with them and carry them to the café, then settle in with a hot chocolate. My dad would get tons of magazines and a coffee, and we'd sit there, sipping our drinks and reading. My dad would always pretend that he wasn't going to buy me anything, because I had too many books, but I'd always walk out of there with at least three or four. I think back to the last few times we went, and wonder if when my dad was pretending he wasn't going to buy me any books, he really didn't want to, since he was worried about money.

Luckily, the romance section in this bookstore seems to

be dead. I plop myself down on the floor, and pull out a book called *The Serpent's Kiss* and flip through it. I love the bookstore.

"Good book?" a voice asks.

I look up to see a very cute boy sitting on a squashy-looking chair at the end of one of the romance aisles. He's wearing a backward baseball hat and a gray hooded sweatshirt.

"Uh, I dunno," I say. "I haven't read it yet." I feel my face start to turn red, and I shove the book back onto the shelf. The only thing worse than an evil grandma type catching you in the romance section is a cute boy catching you in the romance section.

"You should read it," he says. He has floppy brown hair, and his sneakers are untied.

"Why?" I ask. Does he read romance books?

"Because you can," he says.

It takes me a second to realize he's talking about the sweatshirt I'm wearing.

"Ha-ha," I say. "Very funny."

He shrugs and turns back to what he's reading. Probably a stupid sports book or something.

"Just so you know," I say, "I am only wearing this because it's a disguise." There. Take that, Mr. I'm-Way-

Cool. Let him think I'm on some top-secret, government-sponsored spy mission.

"Okay," he says uncertainly.

"I was spying on some teachers."

"What for?"

"None of your business," I say. I drop my voice and try to make it sound ominous. "But all I will say is that it was for a very, very important reason."

"Is that why you're in the romance section?" he asks. "Because you're hiding from them?" He looks interested.

"No," I say. "I'm looking for books." I stick my chin out, daring him to make fun of me. But he doesn't.

He just says, "Do you like to read?"

"Yeah," I say. "But I don't have much time for it now that I'm at school."

"I hear ya," he says. "But I use my reading as a reward, like when I get all my work done."

"I don't ever really have all my work done," I say, sighing. "What are you reading?"

"My favorite book," he says. "*The Catcher in the Rye*." He holds up a book with a plain white cover.

"It has a plain white cover," I say.

"So?" He frowns, his brown eyes crinkling up at the corners.

"So it's probably boring."

"Are you serious?" he says. He comes and sits next to me on the floor. He shows me the book. "It's about this kid named Holden Caulfield. He runs away from boarding school."

I take the book out of his hand, and our fingers touch. I feel a little thrill run through my body. "Sounds like my kind of book," I say.

"He runs away to New York City," he says.

"I love New York City," I say. "Well, I've only been once. But I had a good time." Usually, when my family goes away, we go to places that are warm — Hawaii, Florida, the Caribbean. But a couple of years ago, my dad took us to New York City to go ice-skating and watch the Christmas tree–lighting in Rockefeller Center. Of course, now that our financial situation is probably going to be, um, changing, we won't be going anywhere. Warm or not.

"I love New York too," he says. "Anyway, it's a great book. You should get it."

"I think maybe I will." There's a silence, and it hits me that I'm sitting here, alone, in the romance section of the bookstore with a strange boy. A *cute* strange boy. Who is giving me book recommendations. *The Catcher in the Rye*. Which I am still holding. Does he want me to give it back?

Am I supposed to buy this exact copy? Or get my own? I'm trying to think of something funny and witty to say, when Amber's voice comes calling through the stacks.

"Scarlett!" she's saying. "Are you back here?"

"I'm right here," I say, and her head pops around a stack of books.

"Hey," she says, giving me a big grin. She holds up a plastic bag. "I got a cool sand-making kit at the Discovery Store! What are you doing?"

"Nothing," I say. "I was just talking to—"

I turn to ask the guy sitting next to me his name. But when I do, he's gone.

Chapter 7

On Monday morning in English, I write back to Number Seventeen.

Dear Number Seventeen,

I accept your Four Truths and a Lie challenge, and I am happy to report that number one on your list is definitely true. I saw it with my own eyes, when my friend Amber and I trailed Mr. Lang and Ms. Cardanelli into a restaurant during our off-academy. They were looking VERY cozy, if you know what I mean. Although I did almost get caught, due to a very surly waitstaff.

So I'm done with number one. Easy-peasy.

I'm looking forward to seeing what you have for me next, although I must admit this is kind of weird.

Also, this might be a long shot, but do you know a kid who goes to your school who wears a Notre Dame baseball hat and likes the book The Catcher in the Rye? Kind of tall and cute? I met him this weekend, and I think he goes to your school.

Talk to you soon,
Number Seventeen

In math, I end up with a sixty-five on my quiz. Not so great, especially since I spent all day on Sunday studying. To make matters worse, we grade our papers in class, by passing them to the person behind us. Which means that EVERYONE in the class knows my score. Definitely not a good thing. I would have done much better if we would at least get some kind of partial credit for our work, but nooo. Mrs. Walker says, "If you don't get the answer right, that's all that matters" and so she only gives partial credit on some things, like homework. Which means I can do almost the whole problem right, make some kind of simple arithmetic mistake or use the wrong formula, and end up getting the whole thing wrong. So not fair.

The day gets a little better, though, because there are milkshakes for lunch, *and* it's announced that there's going to be a dance with Brookline Academy for Boys next week. Only they call it a social, I guess to make sure they keep the focus on academics. Dance, social, whatever, it's still going to be fab. Then, at basketball practice, I somehow manage to score two baskets. Rory yells, "Good job, Scarlett!" and even Andrea gives me a thumbs-up.

I'm not sure if it's because I'm getting into better shape, or because I'm having such a great day, but after practice, I'm not even tired and I skip right up the stairs to my room. When I get there, Crissa's sitting on her bed, her nose stuck in a book.

"Good afternoon, Crissa!" I say, spinning around. Even Crissa can't bother me today. I don't even care that I still have to shower before I can tackle the three hours of homework that I have, not to mention brushing up on my math since I obviously don't quite have it yet. I feel like I can do anything.

Crissa sits up and slams her book shut. "Please," she asks, "could you not come in this room shouting?" She takes her glasses off and rubs her eyes. "Some of us are trying to study."

"Sorry," I say.

"Yeah, I'll bet you are." She rolls her eyes and turns back to her book. I want to say something mean back to her like, "Sorry some of us actually have a life and aren't always studying," but at this school, having a life is a bad thing.

"So," I say, sliding into the softness of my bed. Mmm . . . I probably shouldn't be lying on my bed, since every time I do, I seem to fall asleep. I reluctantly sit up. "Are you looking forward to the social?"

"Not really," she says. "Dances are just another way of taking our repressed societal values and imposing them on our adolescents."

I have no idea what she's talking about, so I decide it might be better to just ignore her. And then I realize I might get to see the mysterious bookstore boy at the dance! Or maybe even my secret pen pal. Or at least have him pointed out to me so I can see if he's psychotic-looking. Maybe he has dark hair and eyes and wears a seersucker coat! A lot of times in the books I read, there are very sinister characters wearing seersucker coats.

My curiosity peaks even more on Wednesday in English, when I get two more letters from Number Seventeen.

The first one says this:

Dear Number Seventeen,

I have a confession to make, something that might make you kind of mad. (Yes, in addition to the fact that I'm sending you silly tasks to complete.)

On the second day of school, my friend Davy Pierce and I snuck into Mr. Lang's office in the English department and looked up the list of stranger pen pals. So I know your name is Scarlett Northon. Then, on Saturday, we had an off-academy at the mall, same as you guys, and I asked one of the girls at your school to point you out. I saw you sitting in the food court, eating a taco. You had on a sweatshirt that said I DO IT BECAUSE I CAN and your hair was all messy.

You are very cute, and obviously very smart, because I overheard you talking to your friend about something to do with math. Plus you are a good writer, I can tell from your letters.

Anyway.

I don't know anyone who wears a Notre Dame hat, but I will keep my eyes peeled. And <u>The Catcher in the Rye</u>? That book is so overrated. What's so cute about this guy anyway?

Number Seventeen

The second letter says this:

Dear Number Seventeen,

I am glad you have decided to participate in this game. You have made a wise choice.

Your calling statement number one the truth was correct.

Statement Number Two is as follows:

NUMBER FOURTEEN ON THE SECRET PEN
PALS LIST IS A BOY NAMED LOUIS
MASTERPOLE.

You have until tomorrow to figure this out.
Good luck, and remember: If you choose not to
participate in this task, you will be revealed.

Number Seventeen

Hmm. Well, that's a weird choice of words. "You will
be revealed"? It's like he's going out of his way to make this
seem scary. Although I'm sure he's just doing it to make it
interesting. I mean, there's no way he could know about my
secret. He doesn't even know me.

Here's what I write him back:

Dear Number Seventeen,

I accept your challenge. After all, I wouldn't
want to get "revealed." Ha-ha. Also, I
appreciate your honesty. Honesty is very

important in any relationship, even one like ours, which is based only on letters. And thank you for calling me cute. The reason I was wearing that sweatshirt was because my friend Amber and I had been spying on Mr. Lang and Miss Cardanelli, and it was part of our disguise.

Why were you so interested in finding out who I was, anyway? I wish you had introduced yourself to me. It would have been nice to know if I could return the compliment, and call you cute as well. Right now I have no idea what you look like— do you ever wear seersucker coats?

I have started reading The Catcher in the Rye, and I think it is a very good book. So if you ever do figure out who it was that recommended it to me, please thank them for me.

Talk soon,
Scarlett

"Oh my God," Amber says in math. "You were totally flirting with him!"

"I was not!" I say, shocked. "I don't even know him."

"This is just my luck," she says, her eyes crinkling up at the sides as she lets out a fake groan. "You get a pen pal that you're flirting with, and meanwhile"—she pulls a letter out of her bag and waves it around—"I'm getting letters about this guy's bug collection, and how he'd really like to show it to me."

"Well," I say, "that sounds kind of like flirting. Maybe he's going to ask you to a bug convention or something."

"A bug convention?" she says, sighing. "Doubtful."

"Anyway," I say. "My next thing is that I have to find out who number fourteen on the secret pen pal list is."

"Number fourteen?" she says. "That's me!"

"Well, I'm supposed to find out if your pen pal is a guy named Louis Masterpole."

"It definitely must be," she says. "That sounds like a bug lover's name." She frowns. "Although if his name is Louis, why would he want his alias to be 'Stuart'? You'd think he'd go for something a little more manly, like . . ." She frowns.

"Stone?" I suggest.

"Rafe," she says.

"Draco."

"Granite."

We both burst into giggles.

"What are you two laughing about?" Crissa asks as she brushes by Amber and slides fluidly into her seat.

"Bug conventions," I say. "And bug lovers."

Amber's laughing so hard now she can't even talk.

"I wouldn't start laughing about science if I were you, Scarlett," Crissa says. "Since you should be worried enough about your math grade."

And she's right. I get a sixty-nine on that day's quiz.

"It doesn't matter," I say at lunch, dipping my spoon into my strawberry yogurt. "I'm flunking out."

"It was just one grade," Amber says, putting her arm around me.

"Yes, one grade TODAY, plus the one grade MONDAY, plus not having ANY IDEA WHAT THE HECK I'M DOING." I'm so upset that I drop my spoon into my strawberry yogurt and a blob of it flies up and hits me in the cheek. Perfect. I wipe it off with a napkin.

"We'll fix it," Amber says. "We'll study every night."

"No," I say. "It's hopeless." I don't know how in the world my secret pen pal could have possibly thought I sounded smart talking about math. He's obviously delusional and crazy.

"Look," Amber says. "It's not hopeless. My dad always says that if you really want something, you put your mind to it, and you do it." She pulls a wooden beaded bracelet out of her bag. "Look, here. Take this. My dad gave it to me—he wore it on his first tour of duty in Iraq. He would look at it during a really bad day and it would get him through."

"You don't have to do that," I say, but she presses it into my hand.

"Just take it. You can borrow it. And tonight we'll study. Meet you in the library at seven."

"Thanks," I say, squeezing her hand around the necklace. I feel a little better, but I'm still not hungry. I take a bite of my turkey club sandwich anyway. I have to eat something. Otherwise at practice I'll be all out of sorts. Last time I tried to run around on an empty stomach, I almost fainted and Andrea had to fetch me an orange juice from the vending machine in the gym to get my blood sugar up. Coach Crazy was not pleased. I think she thought I was kind of being a wimp.

"Anyway," Amber says, "do you want me to ask my pen pal if his name is Louis Masterpole?"

"No time," I say. "I have to find out if this one is true by tomorrow."

"Jeez," Amber says. "He's getting a little demanding, isn't he?"

"Yeah," I answer.

"You're not going to do it, are you?"

"I don't know," I say, shrugging. "I mean, the only way I'd be able to would be if I could somehow get the pen pal list out of Miss Cardanelli's desk." The last thing I need is to get caught sneaking around in an empty classroom.

But then the words "you will be revealed" flash across my mind. There's no way my secret pen pal could know my secret. Although he does know my last name, so I suppose it *is* possible. But he started this little game before he knew who I was, so that doesn't make sense. And even if he did know my secret, why would he want to torment me with it? And what would he do with it anyway? Tell everyone at Brookline Academy for Boys? Boo hoo. But if he told someone there, they might tell someone here, and then . . .

On the other hand, sneaking into an empty classroom isn't the end of the world. I'm sure it would be super easy, and if anyone asked what I was doing there, I could just say that I left something in class this morning. I look at the clock over the lunchroom wall.

"I think I'm going to try it," I say, throwing my napkin onto the table and pushing my chair back before I can lose my nerve.

"Try what?" Amber asks. Her eyes get wide and she

grabs the sleeve of my blouse. "You're not . . . you're going to try and find the list?"

"Yes," I say. "I'm just going to run up to Miss Cardanelli's room really quick."

"Scarlett, I don't think—"

But I'm out of my seat and running out of the caf before she can stop me, and before our lunch monitor can realize what I'm doing. The cafeteria is on the first floor of McGinty, which is connected to Howser, so I don't have far to go.

The hallways are deserted, since all of the students at Brookline have the same lunch period. Still, I can hear some teachers talking in an empty classroom. I tiptoe to Miss Cardanelli's room and peer in. The door is ajar, and no one's there.

I try to act like I'm really looking for something, and even go so far as to head over to the vicinity of my desk and look around on the floor. All that's there is a gum wrapper and some lint. Actually, this floor is really dirty. Wow. They *really* should—

I hear voices in the hallway, and I hold my breath, but whoever it is passes by pretty quickly. Okay. New plan. Time to speed things up a little bit. I head over to Miss Cardanelli's desk, and slide open her top drawer. I know she keeps the list in her grade book, because I've seen her checking it off as we hand her letters. This is, presumably, so we don't decide to play a big game and start writing to people who aren't our pen pals. I wonder how she would feel if she knew there were already lots of shenanigans going on with the letters. Probably she wouldn't be pleased.

Jeez, she has a lot of stuff in here. Hair ties, paper clips, stapler, some Tic Tacs (so she's ready to kiss Mr. Lang at any time?). Finally! My fingers close around the grade book. I pull it out, quickly open to the page for first period, and slide my finger down the list, until I get to number fourteen.

Amber Hultenschmidt, and Louis Masterpole. Bingo. And then, just, you know, out of curiosity, my eyes wander down to number seventeen. Scarlett Northon and James McFayden. Hmm. James McFayden. He doesn't sound scary. Scary people have names like Gus Hargrave or Drake Midnight.

Anyway. I slide the grade book back into Miss Cardanelli's drawer, and then start to head out of the room. Easy-peasy.

I'm walking out the door when I bang into her. Miss Cardanelli.

"Scarlett!" she exclaims. She's holding an empty Tupperware container. I guess she was eating her lunch.

"Oh, hi!" I say. My face feels all red, and my heart is

beating super fast. I try to pretend I'm happy to see her.

"What are you doing in here?" A look flashes across her face, like she wants to believe I'm doing something very innocent, but she's not exactly sure.

"I was looking for my cell phone," I say. "I thought I left it in here, but I guess I didn't." I hope she doesn't decide to search me. My cell phone is right in the bottom of my bag, which is slung over my shoulder. Worse, I hope it doesn't start ringing. I have it on vibrate, but she could still totally hear it.

"Oh," she says. "Well, you're not supposed to leave the cafeteria during lunch."

"Oh," I say, hoping I sound breezy. "I didn't know." She frowns for a second, but I rush on. "I'm new, you know?" I shrug and practice looking innocent and confused.

"Well," she says, her face relaxing into a smile. "If I find your phone, I'll be sure to hold on to it for you."

"Thanks," I say. "And I'd better get back to lunch!"

Whew. That was a close one.

The bracelet totally helps. The one Amber gave me, I mean. From her dad. Well, it's either that or the fact that I've been sitting in the library for six (okay, two—but it feels like six) hours with Amber, going over and over the same three math problems. But I think I have the basic idea down, and I just did the last three on my own. AND I GOT THEM RIGHT.

"Yes!" I say, checking my answers against hers.

She gives me a high five.

"Wow," I say, looking at the clock. "It's almost three o'clock already. I gotta get to practice." I start stacking up my books.

"I'm gonna stay," Amber says. "I'm gonna read my supplementals and maybe review for the history quiz."

"Good plan," I say. "Hey, do you want to have dinner together? Then maybe we can go to the computer lab later. I want to Google my secret pen pal."

"Ooooh, you found out his name?" She sighs. "I hope it's something more interesting than Louis Masterpole." Amber was not impressed when I told her that her pen pal was, indeed, Louis Masterpole. In fact, she crinkled up her nose and said something along the lines of, "How come I never have a romance like in those romance books?"

"Yup," I say, slinging my bag over my shoulder. "James McFayden."

Amber frowns.

"What?" I ask, alarmed. "You think he sounds scary? I thought he sounded very innocent, actually. Like some kind of foreign royalty, even. Something very innocuous." I wait for her to notice that I've used the word "innocuous," which means "not likely to irritate or offend." It's one of our English vocab words.

"No, I just . . ." Her eyes dart around nervously, and she swallows.

"What?" I say. "What is it?"

"It's nothing, it's just . . . Scarlett, James McFayden is Crissa's ex-boyfriend."

Of course he is. I mean, nothing can ever be simple, now can it? Does this mean I have to stop flirting with him? Does this mean Crissa's going to hate me even more? Will she find out? Is James McFayden a jerk? Is he flirting with girls now that Crissa has dumped him? Is he heartbroken? Does he like hanging out at family gatherings with Mrs. Bacon? My head is spinning as I rush across campus to the athletic building for practice.

The speed of my head must directly relate to the speed of my legs, because I get to basketball practice five minutes early. Coach Crazy is standing over by the bleachers, and the team's huddled around her, looking serious.

"What's going on?" I ask.

"Oh, good, Northon, you're here," she says. I'm not sure

what's more upsetting—that she got my name right, or that she's happy to see me. Neither is a good sign.

"What's up?" I say. At practice, you don't have to talk the way you normally would if you were in class. "What's up?" is a normal thing to say.

"Andrea's hurt," Coach barks. I look down at Andrea, who's sitting on the bottom bench of the bleacher. And then I notice she has a cast on her ankle. "Oh, my goodness," I say. "What happened to you?"

"I fell," she says. "Up the stairs." She looks miserable.

"I'm so sorry!" I say. And I really am. Basketball is like breathing to Andrea. She can hardly live without it.

"It's not your fault," she mumbles.

"Northon, you know what this means," Coach says. She's marking something off on her clipboard.

"What?" I ask. We need to organize a party for Andrea? Ooh, score! Like a "Get Well Soon" party for the whole class. That would be fab! And maybe I could set up a makeover booth, like a special treat since it's for a good cause. And we could have Sandy Candy, this totally cool thing where you make multicolored vases out of that powdered sugar candy that comes in Pixy Stix.

"It means you're in," she says.

"In what?" I frown.

"In the game. You're starting. Now go suit up; we're going to have to rearrange all our plays." She looks over her clipboard at me. "Since you're so short."

"What?" I say, horrified. "Oh, no. I can't start. There's no way. Isn't there someone else?" I rack my brain, trying to remember if there are any tall girls I know who'd be good in Andrea's position.

"No," Coach says. "There's no one else."

"What about Morgan McGinley?" I try. "She's at least five foot ten. Or Michelle Radichio! She's super athletic, I saw her playing badminton on the lawn once, and it was fierce."

"Northon, what's wrong with you? It's too late to get someone else—everyone has their extras set up already. Now go suit up."

I march to the locker room, my eyes on the floor. Great. How could my luck get any worse than this? I can't *start* during basketball season! The only thing that's kept me going so far is the fact that I'm going to be riding the pine! Isn't that what everyone said? That I'd be riding the pine? I *wanted* to ride the pine! I loved the idea of riding the pine! Riding the pine seemed easy and fun.

I sigh as I slam my feet into my sneakers.

When I get back to the gym, the rest of the team is

standing around, and they don't look too pleased. No doubt they're seeing their perfect season going right down the toilet.

"Northon! There you are!" Coach hikes up her shorts. "Now, listen, take a look at this screen." I realize she has a whiteboard behind her, with a bunch of marks on it. Now, it's not like we've never gone over plays before. But up until this point, I didn't really have to pay attention. I'd use the time to daydream up new color combos to try out during my makeovers, or to go over math problems in my head. One time I even pretended I was writing down basketball plays in my binder, when really I was reading my science homework. It was totally obvious, too, but the coach wasn't going to say anything, because it didn't matter. I was a pine rider—which is what I wanted to be!

"What screen?" I look around. Not all the classrooms have screens set up for PowerPoint. I didn't even know the gym had one. I mean, we've never used it before.

"This one," the coach says, pointing at the whiteboard.

"That's a whiteboard," I say. Maybe they just call it a screen at Brookline, so that no one feels bad. Kind of like when I was little and they used to tell my cousin Kristi that she was really driving her car at the amusement park, when in fact it was motorized and on a track. Of course, this is a little bit different. I mean, all you have to do is look at the board to be able to tell that it's obviously not a screen. And the girls at Brookline are supposed to be supersmart, so I don't think the coach is really fooling anyone. Still, it's the thought that counts, right?

"The screen on the whiteboard," Coach says.

"This is ridiculous," Nikki whines. She pulls her long blond hair out of its ponytail, and then gathers it back up again. "Can we please talk about other options?"

"We've already discussed this," Coach Crazy says. She puts her hands on her massive hips. "There are no other options."

What does she mean they've already discussed it? How come I haven't heard about this? Are they having secret meetings that don't involve me? That's pretty rude. I mean, I don't want to start, but I don't want them thinking I *can't* start. I mean, hello. How mean.

"Coach," I say, raising my chin. "I'm up for the challenge."

The other girls sigh, and a collective groan goes up from the group. They all start talking at once.

"We're never going to—"

"Worked so hard for this year and now—"

"Forget the championship, we won't even get to the playoffs, this is—"

"Quiet!" Coach Crazy blows her whistle and the girls quiet down. "Now listen up," she says. "We're on this team not because we're only going to be happy if we win the tournament. We're on the team to learn about teamwork, and how to become better basketball players."

The team mumbles something that kind of sounds like agreement, but could just be something they do to make Coach Crazy think they agree when they really don't.

"Excuse me," I say. "But has anyone bothered to ask *Scarlett* what she thinks of all this?"

"It doesn't matter what you think, Northon," Coach barks. "We need you. And you need us." She's right. I can't switch my extras. Everything else is full. "Now let's get to work." And she turns back to the board.

Chapter **8**

That night, my mom comes to take me out to dinner. I catch sight of her through the window of my dorm, hurrying across the front lawn and up the steps. She's wearing her long woolen coat with her Burberry scarf, and she's carrying my black carry-on bag, the one I use when we go on vacation. Probably filled with the workout clothes I asked her to bring.

I feel my throat catch at the sight of her. I didn't realize until now how much I missed her. And then I feel guilty for kind of sort of forgetting that she was coming to visit today, what with all the James/Crissa and basketball drama going on. What kind of daughter am I? Especially with my dad out of the picture, she's all I've got right now. When she appears in my room a few minutes later, I throw my arms around her, taking in the scent of her lavender perfume.

"Hi," she says. "I missed you."

"I missed you, too," I say.

"Wow," my mom says, pulling back and surveying my room. "It looks different."

"What? Oh, yeah. I guess because it's lived in." I look at the array of papers on my desk, along with my unmade bed. Whoopsies. If I'd remembered she was coming, I would have cleaned up.

"I brought the clothes you wanted," she says, setting the suitcase down. "And I found a really cute little Italian place where we can have dinner."

"Perfect," I say. I pull my new pink Bebe sweater off one of the hangers in my closet and pull it over my jeans and T-shirt to keep me warm outside. "Oh, you'll never guess what happened! You know how I'm only on the basketball team because I got semitricked into it?"

"Yes," she says. I recounted the horror of being tricked into joining the basketball team in one of our phone conversations. My mom seemed to find it exciting.

"Well, turns out that Andrea Rice is hurt!"

She looks blank. Then I realize she doesn't know who Andrea Rice is.

"Andrea Rice is our starting point guard," I explain. "And since there are only six girls on the team, guess who has to take her place?"

"Wow," my mom says. "So you're going to be starting on the basketball team? Scarlett, that's wonderful." She looks genuinely pleased. I wonder why parents get all emotional about that kind of stuff. I mean, it's just a sport. "Your dad is going to be thrilled."

"Yeah, well, you wouldn't be saying that if you'd seen me play," I say, ignoring the comment about my dad.

"Nonsense," she says. "I'll bet you're wonderful."

"Not really," I say. "Although I do think my layups are improving. I hit four in a row at the end of practice today. I think I was finally getting the hang of it. I would have gotten the hang of it even more if Coach Crazy hadn't been screaming, 'That's it, Northon! Keep it up!' It made me nervous."

"Well, I hope the things I brought are okay," my mom says.

She unzips the bag, and a colorful array of fabrics peek out at me. Reds, blues, grays, and pinks. All my fave colors.

"I've been borrowing things from Crissa." I shudder and my mom laughs. "It's not funny, I have to wash them out in the sink every single night! Plus it's like I'm beholden to her or something. Definitely not the position I want to be in."

As if the devil herself heard me, the door to the room flies open and Crissa comes flouncing in. "Oh, hello, Scarlett," she says. "I didn't know your mom was coming." She paints on a forced smile. "It's nice to see you again, Mrs. Northon."

"Nice to see you too, Crissa," my mom says, smiling. I shoot her a look. Traitor.

"My mom came here to take me to dinner," I say. "And to bring me new gym clothes. So I won't be needing yours anymore."

"Fine," Crissa says, waving her hand as if she didn't pitch a big fit about having to lend them to me. She starts rummaging around in her closet. I roll my eyes at her behind her back, but my mom shoots me a look like *Be nice*. Why is it parents always want their kids to be nice no matter what? You'd think they'd want to look out for their own.

"I'm just getting my coat," Crissa's saying from inside the closet. "It's getting cold out there."

"It certainly is," my mom says, nodding. Crissa is obviously very good at handling parents. There are certain things parents love to talk about, the weather being one of them.

Crissa smiles and stops in front of the mirror. She smoothes her long brown hair back into her headband. "Anyway, I better go. Don't want to be late for student council!"

"Yeah," I say through gritted teeth. "You better go."

"Sorry I can't stay longer, Mrs. Northon. Have a nice visit with your mom, Scarlett." And then she's gone.

"Remind me again why you don't like her," my mom says. "She seems like a nice girl."

"Yeah, well, she's not," I say. "She totally wasn't being nice. She was forcing it that whole time." How can parents be so clueless?

My mom and I pile into her car and drive to a little Italian place about twenty minutes from campus. I order chicken parm and an antipasto, and eat it all, plus three pieces of garlic bread. The food is hot and filling, and the restaurant is cozy and warm. My mom and I talk about clothes and makeup, her job, how school's going. The waiter is bringing us a yummy-looking tiramisu for dessert when she finally asks me about my dad.

"So," she says, clearing her throat. "Have you talked to your dad?"

I pretend I'm chewing a bite of cake and swallowing carefully, even though there's nothing in my mouth. "Well," I say. "No. Have you?"

"I've talked to him a few times," she says. She takes a sip

of her water, and then sets it back down on the table. A ring of moisture stains the tablecloth.

"He's e-mailed me," I admit. "And, um, he wrote me a letter." I don't tell her that I never opened it. "I don't know if I really want to talk to him."

"Well," she says. "It's your choice. But he is your father, Scarlett."

"Yeah," I say, even though this argument doesn't make too much sense to me. He's my father. So what. I mean, I know it counts for something, but does that really give him a free pass to just ruin my life?

"The things that he's done, the choices he's made, that doesn't take away from your relationship, the time you've spent together."

I want to tell her that the fact that my dad and I used to be close doesn't take away from the things that have happened because of him. Losing all my friends. Brianna turning on me and calling me a thief. Crying myself to sleep at night. So what if we used to spend Sundays at the bookstore and watch basketball together? Dance parties and fajitas don't make up for the hurt he's caused me *and* my mom. The worst part is, it's not even really over—things would probably be really bad for me at Brookline, too, if people knew. I'm lucky I was able to switch schools. Otherwise, everything would still be horrible. And it's all my dad's fault. Does my mom think I don't see that? Does she think I didn't notice that the clothes she brought me tonight are all from Old Navy and Target? My dad turned our lives completely around, and I don't think he should just be able to say "I'm sorry" and have everything be okay. It doesn't work like that.

"Scarlett, he feels really bad about what happened."

"I'm sure he does," I say. "I'd feel bad too if there was a chance I was going to jail."

She sighs and pushes the plate of tiramisu toward me.

"All done?" I ask, anxious to change the subject.

"Yes," she says.

So I eat the rest.

The next day in English, I write a carefully constructed letter to Number Seventeen, hoping that he will realize that I will not be privy to his flirtatious ways anymore. No ex-boyfriend of Crissa's is going to be getting me all ensconsed in some flirty letters. Here is what it says:

Dear Number Seventeen,

Number fourteen on the secret pen pal list IS Louis Masterpole. This is a truth. Also,

he is my friend Amber's pen pal. Do you
have any idea why he wants to be called
Stuart? This seems weird.

Any luck on finding the guy with the
Notre Dame hat? I'm almost done with
The Catcher in the Rye and I LOVE IT. It
might be my fave book ever. And I need a
date to the dance, so I'd like to maybe ask
him.

Talk soon,
Scarlett

I spend the rest of the week and the weekend studying
basketball plays, making sure I have chapter three down
in my math book (we're having quizzes all next week),
and hanging out with Amber in her room, gossiping about
the social and talking about books and music and Crissa
and James and Louis Masterpole. Crissa spends most of
the weekend out with her mom, shopping for new riding
clothes. Apparently she's taking up riding. Which is good,
since I've been trying to avoid her now that I know I'm
corresponding with her ex-boyfriend. Not that she knows

that. But still. Plus it's just a good idea to avoid Crissa anyway. She's not very pleasant.

But on Monday morning in English, things take a turn for the worse. Here is what happens:

I get a letter from Number Seventeen (aka James McFayden aka Mr. Life Ruiner), who says this:

Dear Number Seventeen,

Here is your *third statement.*

KARLI MONTESORRI MEETS HER BOYFRIEND ON MONDAY NIGHTS IN THE LIBRARY AFTER CURFEW.

If you *do not find out if this is true* TONIGHT, *the truth about your father* WILL *be revealed.*

Number Seventeen.

There is no second letter. Suddenly, I feel sick, like my stomach is being twisted in a hundred different directions. I take a deep breath and try to slow my beating heart. The blood is rushing to my head, and I lay it down on my desk for a second. Images race through my mind—sitting alone at lunch, Brianna saying I was probably the one that stole that lip gloss, the unopened letter from my dad in my book bag. It's fine, I tell myself, it's okay. Nothing's happened yet. No one knows except for James. I try to calm myself down by taking deep breaths. But it doesn't work. Somehow, James McFayden knows the truth about my dad. And for some other reason, he's decided to blackmail me.

"I don't get it," Amber says, looking down at the letter. We're in the bathroom on the third floor. We're supposed to be in math, but I persuaded her to get the pass and meet me in the bathroom. Usually only one person is supposed to be allowed out on the pass at one time, but I somehow convinced Mrs. Walker to let me go a minute or so after Amber left the room. I sort of screwed up my face into an intense look of concentration and told her I really couldn't wait, that it was an intense emergency. I actually said that. Intense emergency. Which wasn't even a lie.

"What's not to get!" I scream, waving the letter in the air like a maniac. "He's blackmailing me."

"Blackmailing you about what?" she asks, peering again at the letter. "Something about your dad?"

"Yeah," I say. I start to feel tears pricking the back of my eyes, and I head into a stall and grab some toilet paper off the roll. "And obviously it's Crissa. Somehow she knows the truth and she got her boyfriend to start writing me letters and making me DO INSANE, CRAZY THINGS." I blow my nose.

"Ex-boyfriend," Amber says.

"Obviously not," I say. "They must still be together. And she found out that we're pen pals, so she made him flirt with me, and lure me into a false sense of security, and now she's blackmailing me." I blow my nose again, then throw the tissue into the trash can against the wall.

"Hold on," Amber says. "Back up a second. What's the deal with your dad?"

Amber's looking at me intensely, a look of compassion on her face. And I want to tell her, I do. But I just can't. It's not that I don't trust her. But even if she didn't tell anyone, she would still look at me differently. She wouldn't be able to help it. Besides, I'd have to get into the whole story, talk about how much it hurts, how we might not have any money soon, how my parents are living apart. And I don't want to talk about that stuff. It hurts too much to even think about, much less say out loud. "I don't want to tell you," I say finally. "But it's bad. And now Crissa knows about it."

"How would Crissa know about it?" Amber asks.

"I dunno," I say. I slide down the wall so that I'm sitting on the bathroom floor. "Didn't you say her mom's superinvolved in the school? She probably found out and told her."

"I don't think you should be sitting on the floor like that." She crouches down next to me and makes a disgusted look.

"It doesn't matter," I say. "If I get some horrible disease from this floor, like a flesh-eating bacteria, it doesn't even matter, because my whole life is over." It's my own fault. I mean, how dumb was I to think that I could keep this a secret? Of course people were going to find out. People always find out everything.

"Well, you don't know it's definitely Crissa," she says.

"Who else could it be?" I stand up angrily. "Who does something like this?" I'm getting myself all worked up. "And besides, I thought they broke up. Why would she lie about that? And who has their ex-boyfriend start blackmailing the new girl? And how does she know he's my pen pal anyway? THEY'RE SUPPOSED TO BE SECRET."

"Um, I'm not really sure," Amber says. She looks a little concerned, like maybe she thinks I'm about to really lose it. Even though I've already really lost it.

"Well, Crissa will know," I say. "So I'll just have to ask her, won't I?"

I start to push past Amber and out of the bathroom. I'm going to march right into that math classroom and let Crissa know what's up. Who cares anyway if I make a big scene? I'm failing math anyway. I might as well get kicked out of class. Or even this school!

"Whoa, whoa, whoa," Amber says, grabbing my arm. "Calm down there, Turbo."

"I will not," I say, shocked. "My life is about to be over. Now is not the time for calm. Now is the time for action."

"Look," she says. "You have to calm down. Running into math and yelling at Crissa isn't going to accomplish anything. Besides, what's to stop her from telling everyone your secret? *If* that's going on, which we don't even know if it is."

"But—"

"Look, take a deep breath."

I do as I'm told, inhaling through my nose.

"You need to have a plan before you go marching in there, getting all upset and wrecking everything. I mean, honestly, Scarlett, you don't even know what's going on."

"You're right," I say. I keep taking deep breaths, and my heart rate starts to slow a little.

"Write James back tomorrow and try to get some answers out of him," she instructs. "And by all means, do *not* let Crissa know you know what's going on. Who knows what she'll do."

Good point. Crissa is obviously crazy. Blackmailing someone is a serious offense. I think it's even illegal. And plus, why would she be blackmailing me into doing these ridiculous things, such as following Miss Cardanelli or Mr. Lang around? How does that benefit her?

When I get back to math (exactly two minutes and seventeen seconds after Amber returns, you know, so it doesn't seem obvious), it takes all my willpower not to reach out and grab Crissa's ponytail and give it a good yank. But I know violence is not the answer. Well, at least in my head I do.

I'm so distraught over this whole thing that it almost doesn't even matter that I get an eighty-seven on my math quiz.

That night, Amber has a newspaper meeting, and Crissa is at soccer, so I sit in my room by myself, composing a letter to James. I know that, technically, we're supposed to write our secret pen pal letters in English class, but I feel it's good to have things thought out so that I can be really clear about what I want to say. It hasn't been that easy. Wadded-up pieces of paper are strewn around me on the bed.

Here is a sample of what some of them say:

Dear James,

You are a low-down, good-for-nothing, disgusting pig. I hope you get kicked off the soccer team. What kind of unsavory character would . . .

Dear James,

I realize now that you are attempting to ensnare me into some kind of emotional blackmail. I do not appreciate this, and besides, James, I cannot be bought. I have alerted the authorities, and they will be showing up at Brookline Academy for Boys soon, where they will handcuff you and take you to Brookline Juvenile Detention Center for Boys . . . .

Dear James,

I thought we were flirting! Between you and my dad, I am going to have trust issues with guys now probably my whole life; how do you feel about inflicting psychological trauma on me at such a young age? Hmmmm??? I don't know if I'd be able to live with myself . . . .

Obviously, none of these choices works. A is too harsh, B is not true (I don't even know if there IS a Brookline Juvenile Detention Center for Boys, since I made it up), and C is too psychological. Not to mention if I make him too angry, he might turn around and tell Crissa I'm on to them, since they're obviously in cahoots.

I feel like I'm about to start crying, when there's a knock on my open door. It's Miss Cardanelli. I'm still not used to having teachers show up in my bedroom. Too weird. But every night there's one on duty, and tonight must be her night. I wonder if Mr. Lang misses her. Or if they maybe work out their nights on duty so that they have their nights off free to be together.

"Scarlett?" she says. "I was trying to call your room."

"Oh," I say, looking at the phone on the nightstand. "Sorry, sometimes Crissa turns the ringer off when she's studying." She says it distracts her to have it ringing at all hours. Which is ridiculous, because it definitely does not ring at all hours. Well, except for sometimes when Amber calls from down the hall. She thinks it's funny to call my room when she's only a few doors away. But that's only happened once. Or twice. Not enough to have a whole ringer rule about it.

"Anyway, you have a visitor," Miss Cardanelli says.

"A visitor?"

"Yeah, he's in the lobby." It must be my dad, I think, and my heart jumps into my chest. But then Miss Cardanelli says, "It's your cousin."

"My cousin?" I don't have any cousins. My mom has one older sister who has no children, and my dad's an only child.

"Yeah, your cousin James? He's waiting for you in the lobby."

Okay. This is not a reason to freak out. Even though James McFayden, flirter, blackmailer, and possible crazy person (made even more crazy by the fact that he is obviously trying to pass himself off as my cousin) is downstairs in the common room waiting for me.

After I thank Miss Cardanelli for letting me know,

she leaves, and now I'm standing in front of my mirror, wondering what will happen if I just don't go downstairs. Just leave James McFayden waiting in the lobby, looking around, lost and forlorn, wondering where I am. Maybe Crissa's down there with him, and this is some sort of crazy trap.

I run a brush through my hair and pat on a little bit of lip gloss, then slide into a pair of jeans and a pink Dolce & Gabbana top. If he's going to blackmail me, I might as well look good while he's doing it.

Here's the deal with visitors at Brookline: You're pretty much allowed to have them whenever you want, although only immediate family members are allowed in your room. Anyone else has to stay down in the common room with you, unless you get special permission. Which means if I want to talk to him, it's going to have to be in our common room.

I start to get nervous when my foot hits the bottom step. What if he's creepy and scary? Although not likely, if Crissa's all broken up about him. I'll bet he's nerdy. I'll bet he has greasy hair and a big nose and lots of pimples and a bunch of green spinach stuck in his teeth.

I take a deep breath, then peek around the corner into the common room. A guy is in there, alone, with his back toward me. He's standing up near the couches in the corner, looking out the window. He has a backward baseball hat on, dark jeans, and a blue sweatshirt.

"Excuse me?" I say coldly. "I'm looking for James." Even though, you know, it's obvious that he's James. We don't get too many boys around here.

And then the boy by the window turns around. "I'm James," he says. And then I notice the Notre Dame logo on his hat. It's the boy from the mall.

"You," I say, feeling the anger burning inside me. "You from the mall!" Which isn't, you know, the most intelligent thing to say, but under the circumstances I think is pretty good.

"Yes," he says. "Me from the mall."

"Well," I say coldly. "You from the mall, I would really like to know just why it is you are intent on ruining my life." What a great line. I'm off to a great start. I sit down on the squashy tan couch, to show that even though I'm steaming mad, I'm not rattled or anything.

"I'm not," he says. "I mean, I didn't mean to, I—" Good. He's the one who's rattled. He sits down next to me on the couch. I will not be swayed by his rhetoric. (Another English vocab word, meaning "the use of language persuasively." Who said these words don't come in handy in real life?)

"Look," I say. "I don't know what kind of fly-by-night operation you and Crissa are running here, but—"

"Fly-by-night operation?" He frowns. "We're not running any kind of operation."

"Yes, you are," I say. "A life-ruining operation."

"I need to explain," he says. "Crissa's my ex-girlfriend."

"I know," I say. He raises his eyebrows. "I know lots of things about you."

He frowns. "Like what?"

"*Lots* of things." I try to sound mysterious, even though this, of course, is a lie. I hardly know anything about him, except his name and that he used to date Crissa. And that he's a disgusting, heartless jerk. A disgusting, heartless jerk with nice eyes. And good taste in books. But that is beside the point.

"Well, then you'll know that I never would have agreed to this if I knew what Crissa was up to."

"Oh, right," I say. "Like it was all her idea." Does this guy think I was born yesterday? Please.

"Why would I want to ruin your life?" he asks. "I don't even know you." He shrugs.

"Why would Crissa?" I challenge. I try to look in his eyes, but end up looking down at our feet instead. He's wearing shiny white sneakers. *How does he keep them so clean?*

I wonder. My basketball shoes are a mess. Then I realize our feet are close to touching, so I pull my gaze away and look out the window behind him.

"I'm not sure," he says, shrugging again. "Probably because she's threatened. And the only thing she has on you is this secret. How bad is it, by the way?" He leans in close to me, like we're sharing something. I move away from him and concentrate on not looking at him.

"How bad's what?" Still looking out the window.

"The secret."

"You don't know the secret?" I finally tear my gaze away from the trees and look at his eyes to see if I can figure out if he's telling the truth.

"No." Hmm. No dilated pupils. Seems truthful. Of course, he's also very conniving, so he could have some pupil-dilation control mastered. "Look, when Crissa found out we were pen pals, she came up with this idea of playing a game with you. She said it would be fun, that you were new and it would be interesting. She made it out like you guys were friends. So I went along with it. I figured it was fine, and besides, I didn't think it would be fun writing to some random girl, so it gave me something to say."

I narrow my eyes at him. "And if Crissa says 'jump' you just say 'how high,' huh?" Again, not the most original thing to say, but, you know, I'm being put on the spot here. "That doesn't sound like an ex-girlfriend to me." What does he mean it didn't sound fun to write to me? My letters are very witty and compelling.

"It's complicated," he says, sighing. He pulls his baseball cap off his head and runs his fingers through his brown hair. It's all messy and mopsy, falling onto his forehead like that day in the mall.

"Not interested," I say, even though I totally am. "The bottom line is that you went along with whatever she wanted, and that makes you just as bad as her."

"But that was before I got to know you a little," he rushes on. "Before I met you at the mall."

"Oh, right," I say, crossing my arms. "When you met me at the mall, and then totally LIED about it in your letters. Making me think there was another guy, someone else, letting me write to you about how you should find him and . . ." I trail off as I realize I told James I wanted to ask Notre Dame Hat to the dance. Well. Obviously he should know that was before I knew it was him. I debate whether or not to clarify.

"As soon as I realized what Crissa was really up to, I knew I had to tell you. So I got my brother to drive me here." He puts his hat back on his head, and looks me right in the eye.

"How very noble of you," I say, sniffing. "Like I really believe that." Disgusting, heartless, lying jerk.

"It's the truth."

"Then why did you send me that letter today? The one about Karli?" I demand.

"Because if I hadn't sent you that letter, Crissa would have known something was up. She's watching you, Scarlett. She knows what you're doing, and she wants you out of this school." His voice sounds ominous, and for a second I want to believe him. But then I remember who I'm dealing with.

"Why should I trust you?" I say. "And besides, who cares what Crissa wants? If you had any kind of backbone, you'd tell her you were going to stop." A guilty look flashes across his face, and it bolsters me on. "If you ask me, it sounds like you still like her."

An even guiltier look passes across his face. "Like I said, it's complicated."

"It doesn't sound that complicated to me," I say, pausing for effect. "In fact, it sounds like maybe you want her back."

Silence. Aha!

"When she broke up with me this summer, yes, I wanted her back. I thought maybe doing this letter thing would be a good way to accomplish that. It seemed harmless enough." Well, that's that. I stand up to go, but he grabs my arm. "But as soon as I realized what she was doing, I didn't want any part of it," he says. "I have no feelings left for her, seriously. How could I after realizing she'd do something like this?"

The front door to the dorm opens, and James looks alarmed. Voices float through the hall and into the common room before disappearing down the hall and up the stairs.

"Listen," he says, leaning in close to me again. "Can we get out of here?"

I look at him incredulously. "Are you serious? Get out of here?"

"Yeah," he says. "Get out of here. Go to the library or something."

"Look," I say, crossing my arms. "If you're afraid of bumping into Crissa, you have much more of a chance of doing that in the library than you do here. And besides, if you are so intent that this was all her idea, then why are you so worried about seeing her?"

"Because if she knows I'm here warning you, she'll probably be mad, which means she might tell whatever it is you're hiding."

Oh. The sound of a car horn honking comes from outside the window, and James looks at me. "That's my brother," he says. "He said a dollar a minute, so it must have been ten minutes already." He sighs.

"You had to pay him to bring you here?"

"A dollar a minute, plus gas." The horn comes through the window again, twice this time.

I think about it. If James tells Crissa he's not going to write me anymore, she might end up getting so mad she'll blab my secret all over. "Look," I say. "You keep writing the letters. *I'll* decide what to do about it." And then I get real close to him. So close that our faces are an inch apart. "And if you tell her you came here to warn me, I swear, you will regret it. I don't care if she's your ex-girlfriend or not."

"Don't worry," he says. "I won't." He tries to move by me toward the door, and we almost bump into each other. I realize again how tall he is. Really tall. Maybe even taller than any boy at my old school. He looks like he wants to say something else, but instead he brushes by me and out the door, and I collapse onto the couch, realizing for the first time how fast my heart is beating.

That night I skip dinner. I sit in my room, reading James's letters over and over, and trying to figure out what to do.

At around seven, Amber appears in my doorway. "Why weren't you at dinner?" she asks, jumping on my bed. My

Spanish book goes flying off the bed and onto the floor.

"I wasn't hungry," I say. "And James McFayden came to see me."

"James McFayden *what?*" Amber screeches, her eyes bugging out of her head.

"Shhh!" I say. Crissa's nowhere to be seen, but there's no telling when she might pop up.

"What are you going to do?" Amber asks, once I fill her in on the details of the night.

"I'm not sure," I say. I don't tell her that right after James left, I went down to the library and kind of sort of maybe opened one of the windows on the ground floor, so that I could sneak in later if need be. "But I think I'm going to do it."

"You're going to sneak into the library?" Amber's eyes are seriously bugging out of her head now. I'm afraid they might pop out.

"All I'd have to do is figure out a way to sneak in. How does Karli get in?"

"She volunteers there on the weekends shelving books, so she has a key." Amber replies. Not helpful.

"Okay, then I'll just wait until after Miss Cardanelli comes around to check us at eleven, then sneak into the library through a window. We could camp out on the chairs in front of the main windows, and see if Karli shows up to meet her boyfriend." Granted, the thought of spending the night in the dark library is kind of spooky and scary. But I'm sure they must keep some lights on in there somewhere. Plus, I have a hard time believing anyone would catch us. The librarian's name is Ms. Potter, and she's seriously about eighty years old. It's lucky that everyone here is smart enough to figure out how to use the library on their own, because she is not much help at all. She can hardly hear.

"I'm sorry, Scarlett, I just can't," she says, biting her lip. "I can't afford to get into any trouble."

"It's okay," I say. "I understand." And I do. I mean, I can't force her to do something that might get her into trouble. This is my problem to deal with.

"And honestly," she says. "I don't think you should, either."

"I have to," I say simply.

"Scarlett, this thing with your dad—" But I put my hand up to stop her. I know what she's going to say. That no matter what it is, she doesn't care, that we'll be friends. The same stuff Brianna and everyone else said before they laughed behind my back and refused to talk to me. No. I'm not going through that again.

So that night, I stuff a pillow into my backpack, along

with my math book, my science book, and my binder full of social studies notes. I add some granola bars and little packages of mini-cookies and a bottle of iced tea. You never know when you're going to need a midnight snack.

After eleven, we're supposed to stay in our rooms. We get around this rule by having whispered conferences in the bathroom, or waiting until the teacher on duty does her checks before sneaking into each other's rooms. So when Miss Cardanelli comes around to check that we're in our rooms, I smile at her in what I hope is a sleepy way.

"Good night, Scarlett. Good night, Crissa," she says.

"'Night, Miss Cardanelli," I say. Her cheeks look flushed and happy. I wonder if it's because things are going well with her and Mr. Lang.

I make a big show of yawning and telling Crissa that I'm going to go to sleep so that I can be well-rested for tomorrow. She doesn't look up from her book. Luckily, she turns the light out shortly after, and within seconds, I can hear her breathing softly. Not like it matters if she's sleeping or not. She knows what I'm going to do.

I tiptoe out the door and down the hall. It's actually pretty easy to make it out of the building. I get a little nervous when I have to sneak past the door of the Gilbert twins, these two seventh graders who are infamous for staying up all night. They have the door to their room open, and I have to pass by to get to the stairway.

But finally, I'm down in the lobby, and I sneak out the door and run across the street to the library. I turn the knob, but it's locked. Of course. But the window I opened earlier is ajar, and so I slide through it and into the first floor. Well, onto the first floor. I don't even want to think about the fact that I just broke the law. Although, is breaking into the library breaking the law if I don't actually take anything? And is it breaking the law if you're only going into your school library?

Wow. The library is kind of spooky at night like this. No lights. And the new book shelf looks like a ghost. Or a killer. I decide I need to get to the front of the library pronto. It's already eleven thirty, and I don't want to miss Karli. Plus there is a very comfy couch by the front window, and I think if I lie on it, not only is it a central location, but the streetlights should shine in a bit, making it a little less scary. At least I hope it will. Plus that seems like a great place to have a cookie, and these snacks are burning a hole in my backpack.

By the time I get to the front of the library, my eyes are a little bit more adjusted to the darkness, but I'm still having a little trouble seeing. I have to use my hands to move down the stacks of books and maneuver myself over to the couch.

I finally get there, but when I plop down on it, I scream. SOMEONE IS ON THE COUCH.

And that person screams too.

I'm about to run for the emergency exit, not even caring if I get caught (being expelled from school = much better than getting killed at age thirteen), when I realize the person has stopped screaming, and is calling my name.

"Scarlett, it's me," the form says.

"Who?" I say, not turning around completely in case it's a crazy stalker killer person. I look around for something I can use as a weapon.

"Me," the person says. And then I realize the voice sounds more like that of a teenage girl than of a scary killer. So I turn around.

"Amber!" I've never been so happy to see someone in my life.

"It's about time," she says, plopping back down on the couch. "I've been waiting for you forever."

"What time do you think they get here?" Amber asks. It's a little before midnight, and still no sign of Karli. Actually, I don't exactly know what Karli looks like (I've only seen her a couple of times in the hall, and it was just a rush of blond hair and a giggle—in fact, that's the only reason I know who she is. Sometimes I hear Crissa say, "Ugh, that Karli Montesorri and her giggle make me want to cut my ears off, it's sooo annoying.") But it doesn't matter if I know exactly what she looks like. As Amber pointed out a few minutes ago, how many people would end up in the library at midnight with their boyfriend? And then I said, well, what if it's some kind of trick question that Crissa's testing me with, like, some tenth grader *does* meet her boyfriend in the library, but it's not Karli? And then Amber said it was okay, she knew what Karli looked like and to stop obsessing. So I did. Well, sort of.

"I dunno," I say, taking a bite of granola bar. "But I'm sure probably soon. I mean, how late can it possibly get before they show up?"

"True," Amber says. We're both on the same couch, with our feet up, facing each other from different ends. I'm really, really glad she's here, since it's kind of spooky in here. Every time we hear even the smallest noise, I jump. What I actually want to do is scream, "Who is it?" and run out of here, but I can't.

"Hey," Amber says, leaning forward and breaking off a piece of my granola bar. She pops it in her mouth and chews. "You don't think they're going to be making out in here, do you?"

"Of course they're going to be making out in here," I say. "Why else would they be meeting here after curfew?"

"That's disgusting," Amber says. "What are we going to do while they're slobbering all over each other?"

"Ewww," I say. "Do you think they slobber?"

"Yes, I do," she says. "Although I've never been kissed before, so I'm not sure."

"Me neither," I say, and for some reason, James's face pops into my mind. But then I push him out of my head, because when it comes down to it, he is not the cute boy recommending me really good books and not making fun of me for reading romances. He is the horrible, disgusting ex-boyfriend of Crissa and accomplice to a blackmailer. Of course, he didn't know what she was doing. But still.

"You're thinking about James, aren't you?" Amber says, grinning.

"No," I say. I can feel my face start to get hot. "I don't think about total jerks."

"He's definitely a jerk," she says. "But he's really cute, isn't he?"

"No," I lie. "There are loads of boys at my old school way cuter than him."

"I dunno," Amber says. "It doesn't seem like—"

But she's interrupted by the sound of a door opening and a giggle from the other side of the library. Amber looks at me with a panicked look. We grab our stuff and dive behind a rack of nonfiction books on Buddhism.

And just in time, too, because Karli's voice is moving down the library. "It's not just that I don't like my roommate, it's that I don't like the things she does," she's saying. "Like how she's always looking for her bathroom cup. And how I can't really eat microwave popcorn at night because she can't stand the smell, you know?" She giggles.

"Mmm hmm," we hear a deeper, male voice say. But it sounds totally uninterested.

"Blake, are you listening?" Karli demands.

"Yes," Blake says. "You don't like your roommate because of microwave popcorn."

"That is not the point," Karli says. Amber and I cover our mouths to hide our giggles. We're crouched down, and I accidentally step on Amber's foot.

"Ow," she squeaks. Oopsies.

"What was that?" Karli asks. Amber's eyes get wide and we both hold our breath.

"Nothing," Blake says. We hear the squeak of the

couch as he sits down. "Probably just settling. Look, do you want to get started or what?"

Jeez. That's romantic. If any guy ever tries to kiss me by saying "Do you want to get started or what?" I will never, ever kiss him. This Blake must be pretty cute for Karli to put up with that kind of treatment. This is exactly the kind of thing my mom warns me about, guys not treating girls the way they deserve to be treated.

"Yes," Karli says, and we hear the couch squeak again. Probably Karli sitting down next him.

Amber mimes putting her finger down her throat and pretends to gag. It is pretty gross. I wonder if we can sneak out of here now without anyone noticing. Hopefully we can—

"Innocuous," Karli says. What? What's innocuous? His kisses? That's not a very good sign, if she's calling him an innocuous kisser. But really, what can she expect from a guy who says, "Do you want to get started?"

"'Innocuous' means innocent, nonthreatening," Blake says. Then we hear the sound of a page turning.

Amber rolls her eyes and mouths something that looks like *They're such nerds*.

Totally nerds. I mean, they're not even kissing yet. Not that I want them to. Thinking about kissing makes me start to think about James. Which makes no sense. Because I don't like him. Not even a little bit. I mean, he's—

And then I realize what Amber was saying. *They're practicing SAT words.*

Oh. How lame.

And we proceed to listen to them do exactly that for the next two hours, until it's two o'clock in the morning and we're so tired we can barely keep our eyes open. We pass the time by quietly eating snacks and writing notes. But it's very nerve-racking, since we have to be überquiet. Plus, the night security guard, Jasper, keeps walking by the window right over our head. Usually he's whistling. One time he seems to be eating something, and one time he gives a large burp.

When two o'clock rolls around, Karli and Blake decide to pack it up. Amber and I wait until they're gone, then clear up the granola bar wrappers and empty juice cans that are littered around us. Amber looks kind of the way I feel—very tired and disheveled.

And then something horrible happens. When we go to climb back through the window, we realize that although we could get IN by lowering ourselves down, we can't get back up. It's too far off the ground, and even when we move a chair over to stand on, neither one of us has the upper body strength to pull ourselves up and through. We realize we're going to have to sneak through the side door, which is locked from the outside, but not the inside. Which would be fine, except the side door empties right out onto the sidewalk. And so we have to time our escape perfectly, so Jasper doesn't see us prowling around.

"Quick," Amber says, pushing me through the door. We run up the sidewalk and use our key cards to get back into the dorm.

When I get back to my room, Crissa doesn't stir, and I breathe a sigh of relief as I slip between my sheets. I hadn't really stopped to think about what would happen if Crissa woke up when I got back. Would she have asked me what I was doing? Would we both have pretended she didn't know where I was? What if she could tell I knew the truth? I'm not sure if I'm that good of an actress.

I don't have too much time to contemplate it, though, because my eyes close as soon as I hit the pillow, and I'm asleep about two seconds later.

Chapter 9

The next morning, here's what I write to James:

Dear James,

Okay, I did it. I snuck into the library.
My friend Amber came with me, which
was very nice of her. Anyway, Karli does
meet her boyfriend there, but all they do
is practice SAT words. That's very lame.
But not as lame as meeting someone in a
bookstore, lying about who you are, and
blackmailing them. I'm looking forward to
getting my next two tasks, getting this over

with, and never having to speak with you
ever again in my life.

Sincerely,
Scarlett Northon

On Thursday, I get two letters back.
The first one says this:

Dear Scarlett,

I know Karli's boyfriend. His name is Blake
Henderson, and I'm not surprised that they
practice SAT words. He's kind of wimpy.
You'd think that since they're both risking
getting caught that they'd do something a
little more fun.

When I get a car, I'm going to do
something way more fun than drive out to
BAFG just to practice SAT words. And I
will most definitely not charge anyone by
the minute.

Anyway, I'm sending your task in a separate letter. I'm glad you only have one more left after this. Also, I understand you're still mad at me. Is there anything I can do to make it up to you? I'll be at the Brookline social. Maybe we can talk in person. I'm sorry. I should never have gotten involved in this.

Talk to you soon,
James

Here's what the second letter says:

Dear Number Seventeen:

For your next task, you must figure out if the following is true or a lie.

HANNAH WILCOX GOT BUSTED OVER THE SUMMER FOR SHOPLIFTING, AND ALMOST WASNT ALLOWED BACK IN SCHOOL.

You have the weekend to figure this out.
Good luck.

From,
Number Seventeen

My cheeks are flushed. Does he really think I'm that easy? That I could just forgive him? No, there's nothing he can do to make it up to me! Not to mention the fact that he's still obviously so hung up on Crissa. What nerve! Sending me a letter suggesting we meet up at the dance when he knows I hate him. I probably should burn it or something. Instead, I slip it in my bag and read it about three million times before lunch.

Lunch. I'm trying to tell Amber about the nerve of James McFayden, but for some reason, she can't get over the fact that Hannah Wilcox might be a thief.

"She's so quiet," she muses, sticking a straw in her milk. Amber's always drinking white milk. She claims she likes it, which I find very strange. Who likes white milk? Especially when there are chocolate milk and juice to be had.

"Yeah, well, she quietly might have shoplifted," I say. I take a bite of my goulash. Eww. Kind of rubbery.

"I'll bet that's the lie," Amber declares. "There's no way. She's like the most normal, most quiet—"

"That doesn't make any sense," I say. "There's no way that Crissa would give me the lie now. She wants to inflict as much pain as possible. She wants to really make sure I suffer. She's going to save the lie for the very last one."

"You just never know about people's secret lives," Amber says, glancing over at Hannah Wilcox, who's sitting by herself in a corner, eating a peanut butter sandwich and glancing through a supplemental.

"Ain't that the truth," I say. "Anyway, enough about Hannah. Let's talk about the total and complete nerve of that loser James McFayden."

"He has some nerve," she says. "That loser James McFayden."

I nod. "I'm not going to even dignify his whole dance comment with a response. In fact, I'm not even going to write him back until I figure out if Hannah really did shoplift."

"How are you going to do that?" Amber asks.

"I'm just not going to write him back." I shrug. "I have very good self-control." This isn't exactly true, but I can if I want to. "Not that I need self-control to not write him back. I mean, I don't even want to write him back, he's completely—"

"I mean, how are you going to find out about Hannah?"

Oh.

"I'm going to ask everyone," I say. "Someone must know, right?"

"I guess," Amber says. She shifts in her seat.

"What?" I ask.

"It's just . . . I dunno, I mean, if there was a rumor going around about that, we would know about it."

"Well, whether there's a rumor going around or not doesn't really change if it's true or not." I wonder if my mom will take me shopping for a new dress for the social. Something with a swirly skirt perhaps. In pink. Or maybe red. Something that doesn't cost too much. I run through my closet inventory in my head, thinking if I have anything dance appropriate. Something that will make James McFayden so sorry that he ruined any kind of chance he would ever have with me. Something that will make a nice, cute, normal, nonblackmailing Brookline boy ask me to dance.

"Yeah, but . . . look, if you start asking people that question, you're going to be the one starting the rumor," Amber says. "And if she didn't do it, people are going to believe that she did. And if she did do it, people are going to know."

"Well, how am I supposed to figure it out?" I ask. "I can't just ask her."

"I dunno." Amber shrugs.

"Would there be a way we could see her school record?" I ask.

"What do you mean?" Amber frowns.

"You know, like her school record. They'd have it in her file, could we request a copy of it?"

"I don't think so," Amber says. "How could we just ask them for it?"

"I dunno," I say. "Aren't people always getting other people's records? Like on the Web, where you can read all those celebrities' legal documents and stuff." On TMZ.com you can get almost everything. And I know a bunch of my dad's legal documents were on the Web for a while. This super annoying kid named Eddie Newbauer found out exactly how much my dad was accused of stealing, and told everyone at my old school. He kept wandering around the halls going, "Where did that money go?" to anyone who would listen.

"No," Amber says. "School records are like medical records. You can't just get them. Unless you steal them or something."

"Steal her school record?"

"Well, I mean, you can't really do that, you could never do that, it would be ridiculous."

"Where do you think those school records are, anyway?"

I'm trying to sound nonchalant. Because of course I would never steal someone's school record. That would be horrible. Not to mention very dangerous.

"Probably in the office," she says. "But you could never get in there."

"You're right," I say. But the wheels in my head are turning. I *might* be able to get in there, if I snuck in the same way I did to the library. But all I say is, "Well, that's that. I'm going to have to tell James I can't do it. And Crissa will probably tell everyone about my dad."

"Whatever it is," Amber says, squeezing my hand, "it will be fine."

"Thanks," I say. But later, I take a little walk by the administration building. And there's the exact same window setup over Headmistress O'Neal's office as there is in the library. Only this window's already open.

That night, I don a pair of black sweatpants, a black sweatshirt, and grab a flashlight from the supply closet downstairs. I sneak across campus and climb through the office window and into the headmistress's office.

I already know where our files are kept, over in the corner in a huge cabinet. When I came here over the summer to meet the headmistress, she started a folder for me, and dropped it in the cabinet. Of course, it was empty at the time. I wonder if now it says I was in trouble for the whole makeover thing.

I run my fingers along the drawers, looking for *W* for Wilcox. When I find it, I slide the drawer open and reach in, pulling out her file. I hear a sound coming from upstairs, and I jump for a second, before I realize it's just a tree scraping against the building.

I open the folder and run my flashlight down the page. Under disciplinary infractions, it says the following: "Student was arrested for shoplifting over the summer, and after careful consideration, it was decided student would be allowed back to Brookline under the following conditions: GPA stays above 3.0, no school or community infractions. Situation will be revisited after the year is over."

I slide the folder back, shut the cabinet, and then start to panic a little. Maybe I should have worn gloves, so that if anything happens, they won't be able to find my fingerprints. Too late now. The windows in the headmistress's office are lower than the ones in the library, and I'm able to hoist myself out without much trouble. I brush myself off and start running back toward my dorm. No sweat.

But suddenly, when I'm about three hundred feet away from the dorm and freedom, there's a flashlight in my face.

"Good evening, Miss," the security guard says. I can't really see his face, since I'm blinded by the light, but I can see his Brookline Security uniform. "Can I help you with anything?"

Jasper, the night security guard, was perfectly nice about it—he called Headmistress O'Neal and told her that he'd found me wandering around campus after curfew, and he thought he would alert her to the situation immediately. That was the only part that was kind of mean, I thought. I mean, yes, it was a situation, but getting alerted to it immediately? It kind of sounded like something you'd see in an action movie about terrorists or something. That someone needed to be alerted to a situation *immediately*. But whatever.

So then Headmistress O'Neal said, "Thank you very much, Jasper. Please escort the young lady back to her dorm, and I will deal with this in the morning."

Which is how I ended up here this morning, in Headmistress O'Neal's office, sitting next to my mom, who does not look pleased at all. Not even one bit. I think she's mad because not only am I in trouble, but she had to miss work to come down here, which isn't really my fault, since why couldn't they just schedule the meeting for later tonight, when she was out of work? But when I said this, it was met with a glare from my mother, so I dropped it.

"Now," Headmistress O'Neal says, looking down at a paper in front of her. "Scarlett, do you want to tell us what you were doing wandering around campus after curfew?"

"No, not really," I mumble, looking down at my shoes. I considered coming up with some lame story, about how I was going for a jog or something, but I realized they probably wouldn't believe it anyway.

"Scarlett, if there was a reason you were out of your room, a good reason, it will influence whatever punishment it is you are to receive." She looks at me over her glasses, but I look away and at the painting behind her on the wall. "Normally if this were to happen to a student, they'd be suspended immediately, do you understand that?"

"Yes, ma'am."

"But since I know you've been through a lot in the past year, I'm going to write it up and put it in your file. You are on probation effective immediately. If you get in trouble again for anything, one little thing, you'll be suspended. Do you understand?"

"Yes," I say, breathing a sigh of relief.

I can tell my mom wants to say something, but she doesn't. She stays completely quiet as Headmistress O'Neal gives me a paper to sign acknowledging the fact that I'm now on disciplinary probation. Headmistress O'Neal tucks the paper into the file on her desk and tells us we're free to go.

"Thank you," my mom says. I'm hoping that once we're out of the office, she'll stay quiet. I'm so not in the mood to get yelled at. But no such luck. Once we're out of the office, she looks at me. "I am very, very disappointed in you," she says. "And I really hope this doesn't have anything to do with your father."

I sigh. Doesn't my mom get it? Everything has to do with my dad these days. But I don't say anything.

She studies me for a long moment and then looks at her watch. "I have to get to work," she says. And then she leaves without even really saying good-bye.

Amber's waiting for me outside my room. "Scarlett!" she says. "What happened?"

"I snuck into the office to look at Hannah's record. And I got caught," I say, throwing myself down on my bed. "And put on probation."

Amber's eyes get as round as saucers. "Holy crap," she says. "Are you kidding?"

"I wish I was," I say. "But I'm not."

"Scarlett, you have to stop this," she says, sitting down

on the bed next to me. "Whatever it is, whatever's going on with your dad, it can't be that bad. Not bad enough to risk all this."

"But I'm so close," I say. "I only have one more thing left, and then I'll be done." I start taking the books I need for my morning classes off my desk and loading them into my book bag.

"Scarlett, listen to yourself," Amber says. "You're acting nuts. Sneaking around school, breaking into the office, stealing people's personal records!" And a flicker of uneasiness passes across her face. "Besides . . ." She trails off.

"What?" I ask. "What's that look for?"

"Nothing, it's just . . . Scarlett, what if she doesn't stop? What if she keeps making you do things? Or what if she tells everyone anyway? I mean, honestly, is it worth all this?"

"Yes," I say, shrugging. "It is."

I write back to James the next day.

Dear James,

So I found out about Hannah Wilcox. She really did get busted for shoplifting. I found out by a very scandalous method that I cannot talk about here, but let's just say that I'm now on probation. My friend Amber thinks I'm crazy, but I figure I only have one more task left, and then it will all be worth it.

Scarlett

Three days later, he writes me back.

Scarlett,

You got put on probation? You have to stop this NOW. Seriously, this is ridiculous. I'm going to tell Crissa that I'm not doing this anymore. Scarlett, you're going to get in a lot of trouble.

Do you want to meet up at the dance? We can talk about all this.

James

Dear James,

No, I do not want to meet up at the dance.
I do not want anything to do with you. And
please, please, please do not tell Crissa to
stop. I am so close, and I need to do this.

S

I don't receive anything for the next three days.
And then I get this:

Dear Scarlett,

Look, we have to talk. Can you meet me on
Friday night at 6:30 at your school? There's a
clearing in the back, right on the edge of the
woods. I know you want nothing to do with
me, but it's very important that we talk. I
know you have no reason to trust me, but I did
come and warn you about all of this. I tried
to do the right thing. Please, please consider
meeting me. I don't want to see you get hurt,
and I need to clue you in on what Crissa's up

to next. Sorry for the short notice, but that's the only time I can get a ride.

James

I think about it for a few seconds. I'm seriously mad at him still, and the paper I had to sign acknowledging my probation said I'm not allowed to have visitors. But he *did* come and try to warn me, and as far as I can tell, he hasn't told Crissa about it. And maybe he does have some information that can help me. I take a deep breath. Then I pull out a pink sparkly pen, write "OKAY" on his letter, and send it back to him.

On Thursday night, my mom comes to take me shopping for a dress for the dance. So what if James is going to be there? I'm not going to let him stop me from having a good time. Besides, since I'm only on a level one probation, I'm allowed to attend school functions. So I figure I should take advantage. My mom doesn't mention the fact that the last time I saw her, she pretty much was so mad at me she didn't want to look at me. It's hanging over our heads, though, kind of like this elephant in the room that no one wants to talk about.

"What about this one?" she asks, holding up a strapless, flippy pink dress with hearts all over it.

"Cute," I say. "But those hearts are a little *too* cute."

"Right," she says, putting it back on the rack.

"How about this one?" I ask, holding up a baby blue dress that's filmy with a long skirt.

"Nice," my mom says. "Add it to the others." I put it on top of the pile she's holding of stuff I want to try on. It threatens to topple over. "Time to hit the dressing room," she says.

My mom sits on the little bench outside while I try on my first dress.

"How's it look?" she asks.

"I love it," I say. It's emerald green, with glitter over the skirt, and short sleeves. Sooo cute. "This is it!" I declare. No one else is going to be wearing emerald green. I glance at the price tag. Yikes. I'm not exactly sure what the deal is with my parents and money, but I'm assuming that since, you know, my dad is about to go to jail for stealing, things might be getting a little tight.

"Is it okay?" I ask, as I fling it over the dressing room door. I hold my breath as my mom checks the price.

"It's fine," my mom says. "Are you sure you don't want to try on anything else?"

"Nope." If I find something I love, why waste my time? Plus I know the dress I picked is a little on the expensive side. There's no way I'd feel comfortable asking for something else.

I sigh and remember the days when I'd flounce into a store, pulling things off the rack left and right, not even looking at price tags. I pick my jeans up off the floor and slide one leg in.

"So," my mom says, and I stop mid pant-putting-on. Something in her tone makes me think something else is coming. And I'm right. "Are we going to talk about why you were wandering around after curfew?" she asks.

"Mom, really, I don't want to say. But just know that I had a very good reason."

"Scarlett, you and I need to be able to communicate about the things that are going on." I don't say anything. "Your father was asking about this boy who you're going to the dance with. He wanted to make sure he's good enough." She sounds amused, like it was a normal situation, and she wasn't talking to him while he waits to see if he's going to jail or not.

"How does he know I'm going to a dance?" I ask, biting my lip. I think of my mom and dad discussing me, talking about me like everything's normal. "Scarlett's going to the dance" or "Scarlett's doing well in math." It makes my heart hurt.

"I told him."

"Oh." I finish pulling on my jeans and reach for my shirt.

"He mentioned that he e-mailed you a few times and sent you another letter."

"Yes," I say. "He did." Which I never opened. But I don't say that.

"Are you going to e-mail him back?"

"I'm not sure," I say, trying hard to keep my tone light.

"Scarlett, you know you can't just ignore this whole thing. You have to acknowledge it in some way, even if you're getting mad about it."

"I know," I lie. "And I will."

I throw open the dressing room door. "Ready to go?"

When I get back to the dorm, Amber informs me she's going to the dance with Louis Masterpole. This is a very interesting development, since a) Amber has never met Louis Masterpole and b) she has never even expressed any kind of interest in him whatsoever.

"I thought you didn't like him," I say, throwing my bags down on her bed.

"Well, I don't think I do," she says. "Not like that anyway, but he asked me and so I figured it would be fun."

"It will be fun," I say. "I'll do your hair and makeup! And if it turns out he's totally crazy, you can hang out with me."

"Yay!" she sings. "It's my first date."

"Yay!" I say. And we dance around the room.

❋ ❋ ❋

After math class the next day, I stay after to talk to Mrs. Walker.

"Mrs. Walker?" I say, trying to sound serious. "I wanted to discuss something with you."

"What is it, Scarlett?" she barks. She's taking all our graph papers and arranging them into a nice, neat pile. I wonder if it's something she has to do because she's a math teacher. Like, wanting everything to be nice and perfect, just like a solved equation. Is that why people get into math? Because they want everything to be nice and neat?

"I wanted to discuss my math grade."

"Good improvement you've been showing," she says. "You might be able to get a C if you keep this up."

"Yes, well, I feel that when I started at Brookline, I was, um, severely lacking in a lot of my basic skills. So I was wondering if I could possibly make up those first few tests that I did so badly on."

"What do you mean?" Her beady little eyes narrow suspiciously over her glasses, and I almost lose my nerve. But then I square my shoulders.

"I mean, could I retake them?" I hope I sound professional. I hope I *look* professional and responsible too, not like the type of girl who is in danger of getting expelled and has a horrible family secret.

"Well," she says slowly. "That's not something I usually do, especially since those tests have already been given."

"Well, maybe I could be given different tests," I say. "And I could do it in a supervised classroom without the aid of my textbook or help from anyone."

She frowns. "You want me to come up with totally different tests for you, just because you had trouble catching on?"

Yikes. I'm losing her, and so I decide to take another tactic. "Look, Mrs. Walker, I've been working very, very hard. And now that I'm on the same level as the rest of the class, I would never ask for special treatment like this. But I'd hate for my math grade to pull down my GPA, especially since it depends on me staying in this class." I give her my sweetest smile, the one that got me out of doing a detention last year when I skipped gym class so many times the teacher was convinced I'd moved.

"Let's see," she says, looking at her calendar. She has one of those math calendars that gives you a new equation to solve every day. There's some pencil scratches on today's page, like she was trying to figure it out.

"Can you stay on Friday? I have a staff meeting after school, but could you meet me in the classroom at around six o'clock? I'll give you one new test, encapsulating everything we learned at the beginning of the year. I'll add those points to your average, but that's the best I can do." She looks almost giddy at the fact that I'm going to have to give up my Friday night to do math. I think she expects me to say no, but there's no way.

"Of course," I say. "I would be available at that time, yes." I run through it in my brain. Friday is the day of our first basketball game. It's also the night I'm supposed to be meeting James. And since it's an away game, I need to be in the gym and ready to go by seven. Which should give me just enough time to finish the extra credit, run out to meet James, run back to change, and hop on the bus. Yay!

Later, in basketball practice, I'm so tired that I think I might just keel over. Coach notices it too. "Let's go, Northon!" she yells. "Gotta hustle!"

"Sorry, Coach," I say afterward, when we all gather in the locker room for a strategy meeting. "I didn't get much sleep last night and I — "

"I don't want to hear your excuses, Northon," Coach says. "We have to be ready for Friday, and if we're not . . ." She trails off, as if some sort of horrible fate will befall the team.

Andrea sits over to the side on the bench, looking dejected. I swallow.

"Now!" Coach says, blowing her whistle, even though we're all already assembled in the chairs in her office and paying attention. Well, I'm paying attention as much as I can. Sometimes it's hard for me to focus during these little strategy sessions. "Let's go over the plan for Friday. First order of business." She pulls a box out from the closet in the corner and opens it. "Your jerseys. Thanks to the fundraising efforts of last year's team, and a grant from a former student who now plays in the WNBA, we were able to afford new jerseys this year." Wow. A former student playing in the WNBA? How come I've never heard of this? Coach holds up a jersey. It's gorgeous. White with blue and gold on the collar and sleeves. She hands them out, one by one.

I'm number seventeen. I vaguely remember putting that down on one of the first days of practice, when we had to decide what number we wanted to be. I picked it because one time I found the perfect Calvin Klein sundress handbag in the seventeenth store I went into, when I couldn't find anything anywhere else. It's been my lucky number ever since. But now I wonder if lucky numbers can change into unlucky numbers. After all, number seventeen is the number James and I got assigned. Which obviously I should have taken as a bad omen. Hmmm.

My jersey is beautiful. It has my last name, "Northon," on

the back, all spelled out in blue with gold trim. I immediately put it on over my pink T-shirt.

"Northon," Coach barks. "What are you doing?"

"Oh," I say. "I just wanted to try it on." The rest of the girls are looking at me like I'm nuts. "I've never had a jersey before."

"Right," she says. "Well, keep those in your locker, please, and whatever you do, don't lose them."

"Oh, I won't lose it," I say.

"Now listen up," Coach Crazy says. "Friday is our first game." A ripple goes through the team. "Which means we need everyone in top condition." Is it my imagination, or does she look right at me? Hmm. Guess I'm not quite on par with everyone else just yet.

"I'm not just talking about basketball, either," she says, hitching up her shorts. Coach is always hitching up her shorts. I'm not sure why this is—either she buys shorts that are too big for her, or she's lost a lot of weight recently and hasn't bought new clothes. Either way, her body would be much more flattered in a pair of shorts that actually fit her. I wonder if I should point this out to her, but then decide it's probably not a good idea. People are very weird about fashion. They sometimes get a little testy, even if you are just trying to help them. "I'm talking about everything. Everyone has to stay healthy. Everyone has to keep their grades up."

"Keep their grades up?" I whisper to Andrea Rice, who's sitting next to me. Even though she's injured and out for the whole season, she's still been showing up to every practice. She helps Coach Crazy come up with plays to put on the whiteboard, and yells at us to keep us motivated.

"Yeah," Andrea whispers. "One time, like, twenty years ago, the starting center let her grades slip to a C average, and it was this big debacle. She got kicked off the team. Even though it hasn't happened since, Coach lives in perpetual fear that it's going to happen again."

"Stay away from shellfish," Coach Crazy is saying. "We don't need anyone getting any allergic reactions. Stay away from poison ivy." Why would anyone want to head toward poison ivy?

"Someone got it one year when they went home for the weekend and decided to go hiking," Andrea whispers, as if she's reading my mind.

"Also!" she says. "Since it is an away game, please make sure you are on time for the bus. The bus leaves at seven o'clock sharp. That means you must be on the bus by seven o'clock. Not seven-oh-one. Got it?"

We all nod.

The next couple of days go flying by in a blur. Coach is working us extra hard in preparation, and my study schedule is pretty hectic as well. On Thursday, Crissa finds out that I'm going to be allowed to make up the math tests tomorrow, and she's not happy about it. In fact, she kind of pitches a fit. Well, as much as Crissa can pitch a fit. It's like a Crissa fit. There's no screaming or stomping or anything; it's more like a bunch of haughty words and a lot of references about what's fair. She says to Mrs. Walker right in front of the rest of the class that she doesn't think stupidity should be glorified. She actually says "glorified," like I'm somehow trying to be some kind of pop starlet or something, getting glorified for my lack of intelligence. And then Mrs. Walker says it's hardly glorifying, and that allowances need to be made for those who aren't given the same privileges as others. Which is very surprising, coming from her. And then Crissa starts to say something else, but Mrs. Walker starts talking about polynomials, and Martina Miko, this girl who sits in the back and is kind of a bully, mutters "Shut up" under her breath, and so Crissa does. But then later in the library I see her paging through the Brookline Academy Student Handbook and Rulebook for Policies and Procedures, and I totally know she's trying to find something to prevent me from making up those tests.

Chapter 10

"So are you going to be able to hang out at all tonight?" Amber asks the next afternoon. It's Friday, the day of my game, and we're in my room. She's sitting on my bed, painting her nails blue to match mine. Hello, blue nail polish is never a good idea, I know, but tonight's the one exception, since it's one of the school colors. I wanted to do half-blue, half-gold, but I didn't have any gold polish.

"What do you mean? I have a game." How can she have forgotten? I mean, she's painting her nails blue as we speak. I'm bouncing around in my sneakers, up and down, up and down, trying to get myself psyched up for tonight. I'm listening to pump-up music, like "Eye of the Tiger," which I burned onto a CD during math one day last week in the computer lab while Mrs. Walker was in the other room.

"I mean after your game," she says.

"Um, yes," I say. "I'll be back by ten, I think."

"No," she says. "I'm going."

"You're going where?"

"To your game," she says.

I stop hopping. "You're coming to my game? How?"

"Jennifer Benjamin's mom is taking a bunch of us," she says, shrugging. "She got special permission from Headmistress O'Neal. I guess since it's a school function, it's okay."

"Oh, yay!" I say, throwing my arms around her. "I'm so glad you'll be there. Make sure you cheer for me, even if I do something that looks stupid. Maybe that way Coach will be happy with my performance." My stomach flips as I think about people being in the stands, watching me play.

"So do you want to grab some dinner?" she asks, jumping up from the bed. "You should have pasta or something."

"Why pasta?" I ask.

"Because you're supposed to eat carbs before a game. I looked it up online."

"Thanks," I say. "But I think I'm going to chill in here for a little bit, try to calm down." This is halfway true.

The thing is, with all the things I have to do tonight (meet James, make up my tests, and get to the game bus on time), I have no time for anything else. Of course, it involves some planning on my part, and lots of outfit changes. But I think I've figured it out.

Here is the new schedule:

1. From 6 to 6:30, I will quickly finish my math test. I'm going to be wearing a cute blue wrap dress, which I found in the bottom of my laundry bag after my mom took all my clothes home with her. Over this wrap dress, I will be wearing a pair of warm-ups, and under it I will be wearing my basketball uniform.

2. From 6:30 to 7:00, I will rush out to behind the school to meet up with James. I will remove the warm-ups and shove them in my bag on the way over, revealing the wrap dress.

3. At a little before 7:00, I will head back toward school for the bus. On the way back to the bus, I will remove the dress and put that in my bag as well, and I will be in my uniform and ready to go.

Honestly I think I should become one of those time management people who write books about how to manage your time wisely and sometimes even end up on *Oprah* to talk about it. My mom reads lots of books like that. Which is probably one of the reasons she thinks spending time reading romance novels is a waste. In my time management book, I will make sure to allocate time for romance novel reading, and low-budget makeovers. Hmm. Low budget, time management makeovers. What a fab idea.

I also think it's very interesting that I will be able to wear three different outfits—casual, dress-up, and sport—all in one. This is very good for time management. I think I am also going to look in to designing a line of clothes that can change into outfits for all occasions. Then I can possibly tie those in to my time management book, for the busy girl on the run. And they'll be affordable, too, of course. Maybe I'll even get to come back to Brookline for a special assembly, where I'll premiere my line of clothes that are aimed at juniors! How fun!

"So I guess I'll see you at the game, then," Amber's saying.

"Yes," I say. She heads down to the dining hall and I pump the air with my fist and pretend I'm throwing the game-winning shot.

6:07. 6:07 and Mrs. Walker is not here. The clock is ticking, getting closer and closer to the time when I have to leave.

I am sweating. Of course, this may have less to do with worrying about the time, and more to do with the fact that I'm wearing a warm up, a wrap dress, *and* a basketball uniform.

Tick. Tick. The second hand on the clock is moving around, faster than a speeding bullet. And obviously this is not good for my mental state, because I have never used a Superman reference before. Ever.

"So sorry I'm late!" Mrs. Walker says, bustling into the room. She's holding a big sheaf of papers and file folders, and she sets them down on her desk. "I hope you haven't been waiting long."

"I haven't," I lie. "It's okay." Which it's not. Okay, I mean. And why is she holding a stack of papers and file folders? It seems like maybe she brought them in from her car or something. Her face looks all flushed, like she was outside. You'd think she would have just been waiting here at school for me, since she said she had a meeting. And if she was going to go home first, and she knew she was late, why would she stop to bring in a huge stack of papers?

And then Mrs. Walker drops that whole stack of papers all over the floor. "Oh, no!" she exclaims. "And they were all in order, too!" She looks like she's about to have an aneurysm. "Some help please, Scarlett?"

Oh. Right. I bound out of my chair and over to help her. I start gathering up all the papers into a messy stack. And then I have a horrible thought. What if she starts putting them all in order again before she gives me my test? Even worse, what if she expects me to help her? I'm not that good at alphabetizing.

The clock moves over her head. 6:10. I decide to play the basketball card.

"So anyway," I say. "I have to leave for my game at seven, so —"

"Oh, don't worry," she says, waving her hand. "The test will only take you about half an hour."

How about twenty minutes?

"Now, let's see," she says. She starts thumbing through the big stack of papers on her desk. I really hope my sheet isn't in there. She'll never find it, especially now that everything's a mess. "Where could it have gone? Hmmm." She spends the next two minutes looking through her pile of papers, and just when I think she's not going to be able to find it, she extracts a sheet from the pile and hands it to me. "Aha!" she says. "Here you go!"

The paper has a big footprint on it (I think maybe mine; whoops, must not have been watching where I was stepping).

"Thanks," I say, grabbing it and heading to my seat. Mrs. Walker sighs and starts to lay out her papers in a row on the floor, I guess so she can get them organized again. Good luck with that. Yikes.

The test is harder than I expected. There are twelve problems, and I'm supposed to do all of them, then pick the ten I'm most confident in, circle them, and hand it in.

I check the clock. Nineteen minutes. So that's 1.9 minutes for each problem. No sweat. The first problem takes me three and a half minutes. The second one only takes three, but still. Not fast enough. By the time the clock hits 6:25, I only have five minutes to do the last five problems. So I take a deep breath, and rush through them as best I can. I leave the last two undone, and then circle the ones that I've finished. She never said I had to get all of them done, right? And besides, how would she know for sure that the last two weren't the ones I didn't want to count? I feel fairly confident that I got the first ten right anyway.

"Done!" I announce, marching up to her desk and placing my paper down with a flourish. Under my warm-up, I can feel my dress sticking to my basketball uniform, which is sticking to my thighs. Eww.

"Already?" Mrs. Walker asks. She's on the floor, scowling at her papers.

"Yup," I say. I grab my bag and start to back out of the room, before she can say, "But how come you didn't even try to do the last two problems" or, worse, "Hey, Scarlett, why don't you stick around for a second and help me with these papers?" I dash out the door with a quick "Thanks for letting me make that up!"

I slide into the girls' bathroom and into a stall, but then realize that I can't really take my track suit off in here, since there are girls in the bathroom, out by the mirrors. Some tenth graders who I don't know, but still. I can't really just walk out of the bathroom or out of the school wearing a designer navy blue wrap dress that makes me look like I'm going anywhere but a basketball game.

I flush the toilet like I was going to bathroom, then venture out of the stall. I wash my hands (fake bathroom-going obviously must be followed by fake hand washing), and then check my reflection. My hair is a mess from running down the hall — it looks like I've had my head in a blender.

I wish I had time to curl it, but obviously I don't, so I settle for brushing it and reapplying my lip gloss. After a quick swipe of glitter over my eyes, I head back out into the hall and walk quickly through the dorm and outside. There's a little bit of a chill in the air, and I wrap my warm-up suit around me. Actually, it's a good thing I have this on. Turns out it might be a little too chilly for my wrap dress. Of course, a cute pair of leggings would have totally remedied that problem, but I'm lucky I even had the dress.

I check my watch. 6:33 p.m. Great. This gives me way less time than I thought I'd have.

Then I have to wait five MORE minutes for the coast to be clear so I can head into the woods in the back of the school, where James and I have planned to meet. There's a little wooded area back there, with a picnic table and pavilion that hardly anyone uses.

I try to look casual as I stroll into the woods, my eyes sort of glancing from side to side to make sure no one's watching. Once I'm safely in the trees, I remove my warmups and straighten my dress. Hmm. They won't fit in my bag, so I drop them under a tree and vow to pick them up later. Then I walk swiftly to the clearing.

When I get there, James is waiting for me. He's sitting on the picnic table, wearing his gray hooded sweatshirt, track pants, and a totally cute expression on his face.

"Hey," he says.

"Hi," I say, trying to calm my beating heart. There's nowhere else to sit, so I sit down across from him on the picnic table, and try to ignore the fact that our knees are almost touching.

"So listen," he says. "I'm sorry to make you come out here like this, but I needed to meet you in person, and I could not take the chance that Crissa would see me."

"So what is it?" I say. I lean a little closer to him so that he can hopefully smell my perfume, which I sprayed on during my walk over here. He's a jerk, but I want him to see, you know, what he's missing out on.

"First, I want you to know that I'm still really sorry about all this. And the only reason I'm going along with it is because you told me not to stop."

Well. That is true. He did offer to stop.

"I know," I say. "And I do appreciate that."

"Scarlett, I need to tell you what your last truth is, and it's not going to be pleasant."

"What is it?" I ask. Not that things could get any worse. I mean, I'm already close to being kicked out. Hopefully I won't have to risk my life or anything. Oh my God. Our knees are touching. Our knees are totally touching. And he's not moving away, ohmygod, ohmygod, ohmygod.

"Scarlett, Crissa wants you to find out if Amber's dad is really stationed overseas."

"What do you mean?" I ask, confused. "Of course he is." I hold up my wrist to show him the bracelet she gave me. "This is her dad's bracelet. It's been in Iraq and everything."

"I don't mean take Amber's word for it," James says. "I mean . . ." He sighs and takes a deep breath. "Look, Crissa seems to think she's lying about her dad being in the army."

"Why would she—" And then I trail off. Because I've lied about things too. About my past, about my dad. Maybe Amber's hiding something as well. And now I'm supposed to poke around and try to find out. "Are you kidding?" I say. "I can't do that to her."

"Good," James says, nodding. "I think you're right. It's time to call this whole thing off, to tell her you won't do it anymore."

I start to feel a rage coming over me. This was supposed to be my fresh start, where no one knew me. I'm not supposed to be in trouble all the time, running around like a crazy person, doing things that are wrong. And then I look at James, and I start to get even angrier.

"I can't believe you would go along with something like this," I say, jumping up from the picnic table. "I mean, what kind of person does that?"

"Scarlett, I told you, I didn't know she was going to start this whole crazy blackmail thing." He reaches for my arm, but I pull it away. "I wanted it to stop, I wanted to—"

"Oh, I know," I say. "You wanted to stop, blah blah blah. But you didn't!"

"Because you told me not to!" he says. "You told me to keep going, or else I never would have done this."

"No," I say. "You're a really terrible person. I never, ever want to see you again. And I don't care what you tell Crissa. You two deserve each other." He looks like I've just slapped him, but I can't stop myself. "I hope you know that you've ruined my life."

"Scarlett—" He holds his hand out to me, like he wants me to take it, and I see the look in his eyes, how sorry he is, how bad he feels. And for a second, I want him to just put his arms around me and let me cry.

And then something horrible happens. A voice behind me says, "Hello, Scarlett."

It's Jasper, the security guard.

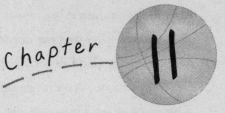

Chapter 11

"Scarlett, this is a very serious violation of school rules," Headmistress O'Neal is saying. She's sitting on the other side of her desk, but she's not wearing her usual school uniform of a suit and pearls. She's wearing a T-shirt and a pair of jeans, because she had to leave her house to come into her office and deal with me.

After Jasper found me, he immediately called her, and she came right over. "Scarlett, you have already been spoken to about leaving school grounds."

"But I was just meeting my friend," I say. Jasper immediately sent James back to his ride. Headmistress O'Neal frowns and her eyes darken. I know what it looks like. I know it looks like I was meeting him in the woods to make out or something. "Look," I say, standing up and slinging my bag over my shoulder. "I'm sorry I was in the woods; I know I wasn't supposed to be there, and that it was a violation of school rules." I take a deep breath. "I know I'm going to have to be punished for it, and I'm okay with that." Well, okay as I can be. "But right now, I really, really have to get to my basketball game, because the bus is about to leave. And if I don't go, we're going to have to forfeit, since we won't have enough players."

"Scarlett, I'm not sure you really understand what's going on here." The headmistress leans back in her chair and shakes her head at me. "Violating your probation is a very serious infraction. You knew you were not allowed to have visitors of any kind."

"But—"

"Scarlett," she says. "Please sit down. Getting in trouble while you are already on probation means you are forbidden from participating in any extracurricular activities, or being allowed to go to any school event." I gape at her. "And until I figure out how we're going to deal with this, you're not going to your game."

I can't believe this. This is the worst thing that has ever happened to me. She didn't let me go to the game. She told me that she would notify the coach and my team, and that she was very sorry, but it was school procedure. Everything is a huge mess. Not only is Crissa probably going to tell everyone in school that I'm Steve Haverhill's daughter, but my mom is going to be so mad. Headmistress O'Neal tried to call her, but of course she was at my game, and her cell phone was turned off. Now I'm not going to be able to go to the dance, and everything's just . . . ugh.

At least she didn't hold me in her office long. She pretty much let me go almost immediately. Not that being back in my room by myself is any better. I wish Amber was here, but of course she's still at the game, at *my* game, where I should be. I've tried her cell phone a few times, but she's not answering. I throw myself back down on my bed, the tears making my face hot. After a few minutes, I grab one of my romance novels off the bedside table. I settle in outside of Amber's room, so that I can be there when she gets home. Forty minutes and forty pages later, my butt is starting to hurt. Amber finally comes around the corner.

"Scarlett!" she says. "Where have you been? Are you okay? I was so worried."

"I went to meet James," I say, and now that I'm saying the words, I start to cry again. "And I got caught, and now I'm in trouble and it's just a big mess."

"Scarlett, I have no idea what you're talking about," she says. "But I think you should know that—"

From around the corner comes the stomping of feet, and another, sort of shuffling noise. Amber's eyes widen, and she tries to pull me into her room. "What are you doing?" I ask. But she's not fast enough, and I get my answer soon enough. "We had to forfeit," Andrea Rice says, coming around the corner. She's on her crutches, and she's followed by the rest of the team.

"Oh, hi, guys," I say, swallowing. I never realized how big they are. Tall girls, these five. "I am so, so, so sorry about this. Really, I didn't mean to—"

"You know, we were really starting to think you wanted to be a part of the team," Andrea says. "We were just talking the other day about how we had you wrong in the beginning, and about how hard you were working, and about how we actually thought we had a chance to win tonight."

"I'm sorry," I say, looking down at my hands. I think I'm going to cry again.

"'Sorry'? That's all you have to say is 'sorry'? We had to drive all the way out there, just to forfeit." She shifts her weight to her good leg. Her eyes are flashing, and for a minute, I get nervous that she might try to hit me with her crutch. The rest of the team huddles behind her, shooting daggers at me with their eyes. "I don't know if you're going to be allowed back on the team, but we just want you to know that honestly, we don't even care." And then she turns and hobbles down the hall, the rest of the team following behind her.

"Wow," Amber says.

"I know," I say miserably, sliding down the wall to the floor.

"I was coming up here to warn you." Amber slides down the wall next to me. "On the way out of the other team's gym I was behind them, and they were furious. I honestly thought they were going to jump you."

"Lovely."

"Scarlett, what happened?"

"I went out to meet James," I say. "And I got caught." I look down at my hands and swallow the lump in my throat.

"It's okay," she says. "Don't worry." She leads me into her room and sits me down on her bed. She hands me a tissue out of the box on her nightstand, and I blow my nose.

"Everything's a mess," I say. "I can't go to the dance, I missed my basketball game, I just—"

"Look, it's going to be fine," she says. She hands me the box of tissues and I take another one. "I'm gonna go get us some snacks from the vending machine, and then we're going to sort this whole thing out. Okay?"

"Okay." I sniffle. Amber grabs her purse and heads out of the room. It's going to be okay, I tell myself. I'm going to tell Amber everything that's going on, including all the stuff about my dad. And then I'll have my mom set up a meeting with Headmistress O'Neal, and I'll try to explain things.

I put Amber's tissues back on her nightstand, and that's when I see it. Her journal. Just sitting there. And then I start to think that maybe if Amber did lie about her dad, she would have something in her journal about it. But I can't read her journal. That would be a total invasion of her privacy. On the other hand, I *do* plan to tell Amber about my dad, so maybe she'll tell me about hers. And then I'll know anyway.

I reach over and run my finger along the cover of the journal, then lift it up gently and peek under the cover. I see row after row of Amber's neat, straight handwriting, although I'm not close enough to see any actual words.

"What are you doing?" Amber's back in the doorway, her arms filled with cookies, crackers, and chips.

I drop the cover of the journal so fast it bounces off the nightstand and falls onto the floor. "I . . . I was just . . ." I take a deep breath. "I just thought . . ."

"You just thought you'd read my journal?" She drops the snacks into a pile on her desk and whirls around to face me.

"No. I mean . . . I wasn't really going to read it, I was just. Look, the last thing Crissa wanted me to find out was if your dad was really overseas."

She looks at me incredulously for a long moment, and when she finally talks, her voice is low and even.

"Look, Scarlett, just because you have some big secret about your dad, doesn't mean I do." She marches over to her bulletin board and pulls down a picture and shoves it in my face. It shows a smiling man in army fatigues, his arm around Amber. "See now?"

And then I realize there was no lie. Amber was telling the truth, and Crissa set it up so that I would think she was lying. She set up this whole game so that I'd have to do all these horrible things, get caught and almost kicked out of school, and then at the end, have to accuse my friend of being a liar. And if I was thinking straight, if I wasn't so caught up in my own anger and lies, I would have realized that.

"Amber, I'm so sorry, I just—"

"Scarlett," she says. "Please leave."

And so I do.

By the time I get to my room, I'm about to explode. Everything is a complete and total mess. And all because of Crissa! Never mind that I was the one who decided to play along with her little game. Never mind that I was the one who broke into the office. Never mind that I was the one who snuck off campus. If she hadn't made James start writing me those letters, I never would have done any of these things in the first place! Honestly, who does she think she is? She's had it out for me from day one for NO REASON. I've been NOTHING BUT NICE to her this whole time.

When I get to my room, I throw open the door, ready to explode. Crissa's sitting there on her bed, talking to her mom on her cell phone.

"Yes, Mother," she says. "I will make sure that Mrs. Walker knows that." She's painting her nails on her nightstand, the phone cradled against her shoulder. She's painting them clear. Who paints their nails clear?

"Can I talk to you for a second?" I ask, tapping my foot. I cross my arms against my chest.

She holds up her finger, like *one minute*. "Yes," she says into the phone. "I called Saddlecrest about the riding lessons, and they said Saturday mornings at eight are the only available time. But I think if I rearrange a few things, it shouldn't be a problem."

"It's kind of important," I say, louder. I don't care that she's talking to her stupid mom about her stupid riding lessons or about her stupid math grade. I don't care that I'm being completely rude.

"I have to go, Mom," Crissa says, sighing. "Scarlett's here and she's going on and on about something." She pushes the end button on her phone and throws it down on the bed. "What is it?"

"Why did you make James do that?" I demand. No more Miss Nice Guy. Who cares if no one likes me when they find out about my dad? It's not like anyone does anyway.

"What do you mean?" She puts an innocent look on her face, but I see the panic that passes across it for a second, and I can tell it's not a real innocent look, but a fake one, carefully constructed to make sure she looks innocent when she really isn't.

"I mean why did you start making me do all those things!" I throw my hands up in the air. "I know you did it. I know you told James to do it, he told me. All about it. How you tricked him into thinking it would be a cool game for him to play, and then how you started making him do it. I've known all along! And I played along with it because I was afraid about the stuff about my dad coming out, BUT I AM NOT AFRAID ANYMORE." I'm pacing around the room now, throwing my hands in the air like some kind of crazy person.

"Look, Scarlett," she says, jumping off the bed and

smoothing her hair down with her hand. She checks her reflection in the mirror over her dresser. "What you decided to do with those letters was your own business. It had nothing to do with me."

"Why would you do that? There's no reason for it! You hardly even know me!"

"You know what?" she says, whirling around. "Have you ever stopped to think that maybe you deserved it, marching in here with your expensive clothes and your stupid makeovers?"

I gasp. "I don't wear expensive clothes anymore, and MY MAKEOVERS ARE NOT STUPID!"

"And thinking you were so mysterious, making everyone think you came here because you were so smart, when really, it was just because of some stupid thing with your dad stealing!"

"So you're admitting it!" I say.

"You know, Scarlett, a lot of people here work hard to be here. They don't just get a free ride."

"I *have* been working hard," I say.

"Whatever," she says. She gets up off the bed and heads to the closet, where she pulls a sweater off a hanger and pulls it over her head. She shoves her feet into her sneakers.

"Oh, no," I say. "You're not leaving. We're going to talk about this, whether you like it or not."

"Oh, Scarlett," she says. "You don't get it, do you? You're lazy and rude and I'm sorry I have to even look at you."

And then she walks out of the room, and leaves me standing there with my mouth open.

I'm so upset that I don't sleep at all that night. Or for most of the weekend. I spend most of my time in the library, avoiding Crissa and studying. And studying. And studying. Math, science, English reading. I keep my brain moving so that I won't have to think about what happened on Friday, and about how pathetic it was to give up everything I've worked for.

On Tuesday morning in English, I get the following letter:

Dear Scarlett,

I'm so sorry for what happened on Friday. In fact, I'm sorry about this whole thing. I never should have even started it up. It was stupid. I can't believe a lot of the things I'm doing lately.

I hope you can forgive me. Can you? Please circle one. Yes. No. Maybe.

James

I send him back a blank piece of paper.

Chapter 12

On Thursday afternoon, I head slowly to the headmistress's office for the meeting with my mom. When I get there, I can hear them laughing through the door. I take this as a good sign, until I walk into the room and the laughing stops. Well, okay then.

I take a seat and decide that my new plan is to be completely and totally responsible, and to keep my cool. One of our vocab words in English this year was "equanimity," and that's what I'm going to be: equaniminous. It means very centered and stable.

"Hello, Scarlett," Headmistress O'Neal says, pointing to the chair in front of her desk. "Take a seat."

"Hello," I say. I'm wearing a long gray skirt and a white

blouse, both of which were borrowed from Amber, and look quite conservative if I do say so myself. Of course, I borrowed them before we had our fight, and I have a feeling if she knew I was wearing them, she would not be pleased. Over the past few days, I've tried to talk to her about a bazillion times and she just ignores me. The worst was yesterday, when I approached her while she was coming out of the newspaper office. She pushed right by me without saying anything except "I want my bracelet back."

"Hi, Mom," I say.

"Hello," she says shortly. Not a good sign.

"Now, I was talking with your mother before you got here, and I've filled her in on all the details." She clears her throat. "My decision as far as disciplinary action is to suspend you for three days, keep you on probation, and let you know that if you break one more school rule, even if it's something very small, you will be asked to leave Brookline. No questions asked. This means *any* school rule."

I swallow. "Okay."

"You will be allowed to play basketball for the rest of the year, provided your grades stay high." She looks down at her papers. "From what I can tell, you're doing fine here academically, so that doesn't seem like it should be a problem."

"Yes," I say. Well, until I possibly screwed up my math grade because of this whole thing, but I don't bring that up.

Headmistress O'Neal rises from behind her desk and smoothes down her suit. "Well," she says. "Now that that's taken care of, I'll give you a moment alone with your mother."

She nods to us both, and then exits the room.

The momentary relief I felt at being let off without too much of a punishment dissolves when I realize now I'm going to have to deal with my mom, who's been silent up until this point. Seriously, she hasn't said one word.

There's a moment of silence, and we don't say anything for a second.

"Scarlett—" my mom starts at the same time I say, "Mom—"

Then we both stop.

"Mom, look," I say. "I'm so sorry that I did this. And it won't happen again."

"You said that last time, Scarlett," she says, pursing her lips. "I thought that bringing you to Brookline would allow you to have more fun, to focus more on your studies and on friendships, things that you should be focusing on at your age."

"I know," I say. "I have been focusing on those things. I—"

"But maybe I was wrong." I look down at her lap, and see that she's wringing her hands. Oh my God. I've upset my mom so much that she's wringing her hands. She never does that, unless she's super, super upset.

"You weren't wrong," I try again. "I just—"

"No, Scarlett, I was. I thought that allowing you to go here would allow you to get away from all the stuff with your dad, but now I think you're just using it as an excuse to not deal with what's going on."

I gasp. "Mom, no! I know I've had some tough times, but that doesn't mean—"

She holds her hand up. "Scarlett," she says. "Please. Sneaking off campus to meet boys, literally ignoring your father. You're acting out and not dealing with your life." And then I realize she's right. I think about the letter my dad sent me, still at the bottom of my bag, unopened.

"You're right," I say, and now the tears are coming strong. "Mom, I'm so sorry, I never wanted to disappoint you."

"Scarlett, honey, you're not disappointing me. I love you and I just want you to be happy. But part of being happy means dealing with the things that are going on, not just ignoring them."

"Mom, I won't—"

"Scarlett, please." She sighs. "I need some time to think about all of this."

And then she gets up and leaves.

At basketball practice, no one will even look at me. It's my first day back since I missed the game, since we were waiting to hear if I could still play. Coach Crazy has a big meeting with everyone at the beginning, and all she says about my little, uh, situation is that it's been decided that I'll be allowed to play on the team. I have a feeling that if it were up to her, she would not have let me back on the team, and for a second, I feel like everyone is going to start booing. You'd think they'd be relieved and excited, since without me, they only have four people. But Andrea is going to be getting her cast off next week, and before that, we only have one more game. The team is so mad at me, it seems like they'd rather forfeit that game than let me play.

"I'm really sorry, you guys," I say after the meeting. "I'm going to work really hard to make it up to all of you, and it won't happen again. I won't let you down."

But they don't even respond.

Coach Crazy works me hard in practice. She keeps yelling at me, "Northon, pick it up! Pick it up, Northon!" and "Northon, look alive!"

❊ ❊ ❊

Over the next five days, James sends me two more letters, apologizing for his part in the whole Crissa debacle. In the last one, he tells me it will be the last note he writes me but that if I ever decide I want to talk, I can write to him. I send back blank pieces of paper both times.

I get a total of five hours of sleep. Honestly. Okay, maybe not exactly five hours, but that's what it feels like. It's probably more like twenty-five or thirty. But still. Five or six hours a night is definitely not good for me. I almost fell asleep the other day in science, and I came this close to burning my hair on a Bunsen burner, which would not have been a good look.

I'm spending most of my time studying for the math test, going over problem after problem. Everything we've done in this unit, along with everything we're about to do in the next three or four units. I'm also working myself hard in practice, running my butt off, even before Coach Crazy is yelling at me. And I'm staying after practice too, taking practice shots and working on free throws.

On Tuesday, Andrea grudgingly says "Nice job" to me as she passes me on the way out of the gym. My face flushes.

On Friday, we have a big unit test in math, and our

second basketball game of the season. It's also the day of the Brookline social, but as I'm not allowed to go to that, and wouldn't have a date even if I was, I'm pretty unconcerned. I don't sleep the night before, because I'm up trying to memorize equations, and also because I'm too nervous. At breakfast, I fill my plate with pancakes, sausage, bacon, and two pieces of toast with jelly.

In math, I wait expectantly as Mrs. Walker starts passing out the tests. One row over, Crissa is inspecting her nails like she's not nervous at all.

The first three questions are easy—they're from our review sheets, and I've gone over them five million times. The next two are new, but still pretty easy, since they use the same formula as the first two. The last five are a little more complicated, but I'm pretty sure I get those right, although there is a tricky situation with a decimal that almost makes me get the last one wrong.

Then it's time for the extra credit questions. There are ten extra credit questions, but definitely not enough time in the period to do all of them. We're supposed to pick out the ones we think we have the best chance of getting right, and do them first.

There are two that are pretty easy, and I do those first. The other ones are from units we haven't gone over yet, so

I do those as best I can. I'm working on my sixth problem when the bell rings. Crap. I finish it as quickly as I can, figuring a rushed answer that might be right is better than no answer at all.

"How did you do?" Crissa asks me on the way out.

And I look her right in the eye. "Fabulous."

I get called down to the headmistress's office later that afternoon, which is quite upsetting. Why do they keep calling me down there?! There's no way I can be in trouble, is there? Unless Crissa has decided to step up her "I hate Scarlett" campaign and frame me for some sort of crime that I haven't committed.

"Hi, Scarlett," the office secretary says when she sees me walk through the door. Hmm. I doubt it's a good sign when the secretary knows you by name. There's no way that can be a good thing. It's like she knows you as one of the bad kids or something. "You can go right in."

I walk into the office, checking the clock nervously. There are only two hours until my game, and I want to get there at least an hour early, so that I can make sure I'm all suited up, and that I don't have a repeat of last time.

When I knock on the door to the headmistress's office, a voice on the other side calls "Come in!"

My mom is sitting in front of the desk. Headmistress O'Neal is nowhere to be found.

"Mom!" I exclaim. I am so happy to see her that I run up and throw my arms around her. I inhale her scent, a combination of perfume and peppermint gum. But then I have a horrible thought. Maybe my mom is here because she wants to take me out of Brookline.

"Hi," she says, giving me a squeeze.

"Where's the headmistress?" I ask.

"She's not here." She sits down in one of the big leather chairs in front of the desk. She smoothes her skirt and gestures toward the other chair. I sit. "She said we could have the office to ourselves."

I swallow around the lump in my throat. The headmistress probably wanted us to have the room to ourselves, so that when my mom tells me she's taking me out of Brookline, she doesn't have to witness it. She probably thinks I'm going to make a scene or something, with a big tantrum and lots of yelling.

"That was nice of her," I say.

"It was." My mom nods and clears her throat. "Scarlett, I'm sorry for yelling at you the other day."

"It's okay," I say. "I deserved it. I shouldn't have snuck off campus like that."

"I realized that I was putting my own stuff on you," she says. "It's just that I met your father when I was so young, and I just . . . I don't want the same thing happening to you."

"I understand." I say, looking down at my hands. I wonder if I'll have to leave school immediately, like on TV when someone gets fired and they have to pack up their stuff in a box. And then security has to escort them out. Is Jasper going to be asked to walk me to my mom's car? I probably won't even be able to play in the basketball game tonight. All those suicides and shooting drills for nothing. Maybe I'll be able to play on the team at my old school.

"But I should have just let you find your own way," my mom says. "I shouldn't have tried so hard to keep you from things that I thought would hurt you. Maybe by keeping you from that stuff, it just made you want to avoid those things more, I just don't—"

"Mom!" I say, holding my hands up. "No. You did the right thing. I'm the one who messed up. I'm the one who was breaking the school rules. I shouldn't have done that. I let you down, I let my friends down, I let my basketball team down. I let myself down." A tear slips out my eye and down my cheek, and I wipe it away with the back of my hand.

"You made a mistake, that's all," my mom says. She

reaches over and squeezes my hand. "And I'm really proud of the grades you've gotten here. Headmistress O'Neal was telling me about how well you're doing, especially in English, which she says is one of their most challenging programs."

"Thanks." I'm really crying now, the tears slipping down my cheeks. "It's just really hard, you know, Mom?"

"I know," she says, putting her arms around me.

"I really miss him," I say into her shirt.

"I miss him too," she says. And we sit there, like that, both of us crying, for a long time.

On my way over to Gym A for the game, I stop by Amber's room and knock on the door. She opens it, takes one look at me, and starts to shut it.

"Wait," I say. "I wanted to give you back your bracelet." I hold it out, along with the romance novel she let me borrow the first night we hung out.

"Thanks," she says, taking it back. "Is that all?"

"No," I say. "I . . . Look, I'm sorry, and I'm sure you've heard, but I'm not allowed to go to the dance."

"So?" she says.

"So, I was thinking that if you were still going, you could wear my dress." I hold out the emerald green dress that I bought when I went shopping with my mom. "And I could probably do your hair and makeup if you want. You know, before my game."

She stares at the dress for a really long time, and then opens the door. "Come in."

Twenty minutes later, Amber looks like a gorgeous princess.

"You look gorgeous," I tell her.

"Thanks," she says, twirling around.

"Amber, I'm so sorry that I looked in your journal." I look down at my hands. "Look, the thing about my dad . . . My dad is Steve Haverhill."

"Steve Haverhill?" She frowns. "Why does that name sound familiar?"

"Because he stole money from his company, and it's this big scandal."

"Oh!" she says. "Right, from WebWorkz. He's your dad?"

"Yeah," I say. "And the reason I came here was because it was a total scandal at my other school, everyone knew, and there was this girl, Brianna, and a situation with a lip gloss and . . . anyway. I didn't want anyone here to know. But now everything's all screwed up, so it doesn't even matter." I'm crying now. "And you're the best friend I have here, and to think that I messed it up over something so stupid is just . . ."

"It's okay," she says, her face softening. "It'll be okay." And she pulls me close and I'm trying not to cry on the dress she's wearing, and somehow, I know she's right. It's going to be okay. Because you know what? It usually always is.

When I get to the gym, my locker is jammed, which is definitely not a good omen for the night. I've never actually believed that whole thing about signs or whatever, but it's enough to rattle me.

"Come on," I say, trying to move the dial on the combination lock so that it will open.

"What's the problem here?" Andrea asks. Taylor is standing behind her—they're both already dressed in their uniforms.

"I can't get my locker open," I say.

She rolls her eyes at me. I know she's probably thinking, *Okay, what other kind of trouble can she possibly bring here?* "I know, I know," I say. "It's always something with me."

Taylor steps forward and smacks the locker with her fist. It pops open.

"Thanks," I say, reaching in and pulling out my uniform. I run my fingers over the stitching on the back, which says NORTHON in blue letters. A little thrill runs through my body. I'm on the team. And I have a chance to make things better.

"You're welcome," Taylor says.

"You better bring it tonight, Northon," Andrea says.

"Oh," I say. "I will."

Wow. I never knew what it would be like to be out here like this, in front of all these people, under the lights. Well, not really under the lights, since we're in the gym, not outside in the dark or anything. The crowd is insane. It seems like maybe the whole school has come out to watch the game. And of course everyone's parents are here, and even some grandparents and friends from home. I spot my mom sitting up in the bleachers. She's sitting with Headmistress O'Neal, and they wave to me as I take my place on the bench.

They do the starting lineups, and when my name is called, a huge thrill moves through my body as the crowd cheers.

"Now, listen up," Coach Crazy says in the huddle. "We have a chance to win this. Cardmore is deep, so we're going to have to do our best to keep our legs fresh." Is it my imagination, or does she look over at me? Note to self: Conserve energy. "Play smart, and work together. Play the defense as much as you can. Scarlett, stay on number twelve, Ramirez. She has a wicked outside shot."

"Right," I say.

She gives some instructions to Nikki and Taylor, and then it's time for the game to start.

We put our hands in a big pile in the middle of our huddle, yell "one, two, three, TEAM!" and then break. We're really going to have to work on that cheer. The soccer one is way better.

I get off to a shaky start, missing the opening tip, which sails right into the hands of Ramirez, the girl I'm supposed to be guarding. She takes it to the hoop, and slides it right in, giving Cardmore a two-to-nothing lead.

"That's okay, Northon," Taylor says to me as we head back down the floor. "Just be careful and don't let it get in your head."

Right.

But the next five minutes aren't any better. I'm having trouble keeping up with Ramirez, and soon, Cardmore gets out to a twelve-to-six lead. But then, as we're running down the court, I notice that Ramirez has a little bit of trouble if I guard her on her left side. She can't run as fast, and she doesn't have a good grip on the ball. I'm able to knock it out of her grasp, and Nikki grabs it, running back up and getting an easy layup.

"Good job, Scarlett!" Andrea screams from the sidelines.

By the time halftime rolls around, I'm exhausted. You'd think all the practices would have brought my fitness level up, but I guess not.

In the locker room, Coach is not happy.

"They're beating you down the field almost every possession," she says. "You need to hustle, hustle, hustle. And play the defense."

Things get a little better in the second half. I'm more used to the way Ramirez is moving, and I'm able to guard her better. I even make a basket. Then I get fouled, and make both my free throws, which means I've scored four points for the team.

Nikki and Taylor are on fire. They seem to have found their rhythm in the second half, and they're hitting shot after shot. Finally, I look up to see the scoreboard and realize we're within four points with only two minutes left. Another girl on the Cardmore team, Smith, takes a shot and it rims out, right into my hands. I dribble it down the court, Ramirez hot on my heels. I pass it off to Rory, who sets her feet and shoots. I hold my breath as I watch it swirl around the rim and then finally fall through the hoop. Now we're only two points down. On the next possession, Cardmore commits an offensive foul against Taylor, and she nails both her free throws. Tie game.

Cardmore misses their next shot, and then we score. We're up by two, and the crowd is going wild. I am doing my best to keep up with the group, but my fitness is still not up to their level. I never realized games were so physically demanding.

There's only sixteen seconds left in the game, we're two points up, and Cardmore has the ball. They call a time-out.

"Now, listen," Coach Crazy says once we're in the huddle. For someone so crazy, she is surprisingly lucid during the games—although I can still hear her from the sidelines, yelling my name, the same way she does in practice. "They're going to give it to Ramirez. Northon, you have to stay on her. The rest of you, make sure you don't leave anyone open. And if they score, everyone should be ready to race back down the court. We might have a chance to score again."

We do our "one, two, three, TEAM" thing again, and then we're on our way.

Just like Coach Crazy predicted, they give the ball to Ramirez. Sixteen seconds, fifteen. The rest of my team is guarding the other players, and Ramirez is dribbling the ball, running down the clock. Fourteen seconds, thirteen. When there's eight seconds left, she starts to make a move. She dribbles around me, and gets by. But she takes just a split second too long to set her feet before she takes the shot, and I'm able to get halfway in front of her. I see the ball leave her fingers, and I put my hand up to try and block the shot.

Everything moves in slow motion as I feel my hand brush the rough surface of the ball. And then I watch as it goes sailing out of bounds. And then everything goes back to normal speed as my team piles on me, screaming and cheering. We won. The crowd is going wild. I'm laughing and hugging everyone and it's the best feeling I've ever had.

And then, up in the bleachers, through a space in the crowd, I see Amber. She's jumping up and down, wearing my green dress, cheering along with everyone else. I catch her eye, and then, very slowly, she turns her hand into a thumbs-up.

When I get back to my room, the dorm is deserted. Everyone's at the dance. But it's okay. I do a little dance around my room, feeling better than I have in days. My mom took me out for pizza after the game and it sloshes around in my stomach.

After I take a nice long, hot shower, I decide I've earned myself a little R & R. So I pull on a comfy pair of pajama pants, a fleece shirt, and grab *The Catcher in the Rye* off my shelf. I open a huge bag of peanut M&M's, snuggle down into my comforter, and get ready for a night by myself. Well, at least until Amber gets home and can tell me all about Louis Masterpole. And maybe about James. Just, you know, if he was at the dance. And if he asked about me. Not that I care that much, but just, you know, out of curiosity. I swallow the lump in my throat and force myself to concentrate on my book.

It's about half an hour later when Crissa appears at our door.

She's carrying a bag of books and is dressed in jeans and a navy blue hooded sweatshirt.

"James was looking for you," she says. My heart starts beating very fast, but I force myself not to react and keep my eyes on my book. I don't care if he's looking for me. The jerk. And I certainly will not let Crissa see me react to this piece of news. I will not talk to her. I will not look at her. I will not—

"Why was he looking for me?" I ask.

"I dunno," she says, shrugging. "I think he wants to talk to you, apologize for this whole thing. I saw him standing outside the gym on my way back from the library."

"You didn't go to the dance?" I ask. I thought everyone was there except for me. And then I remember Crissa's remark about the dance being an archaic mating ritual or something.

"Too much studying to do," she says. "And I have a riding lesson early tomorrow, so that's cutting into my study time."

I roll my eyes and go back to reading my book.

And that's when it happens.

Crissa starts crying.

She plops right down on her bed, her back toward me, and her shoulders start shaking. She's not even making that much noise, but she's crying hard, one of those silent cries, where you almost can't catch your breath.

Oh, jeez. I sigh and set my book gingerly on the bed and walk over toward her. "Uh, what's wrong?" I ask.

"Nothing," she says, quickly wiping the tears away from her eyes.

"There must be something," I say. "You're crying." I sit down on her bed next to her.

"Like you care," she says. There's a wet spot on her sleeve.

"Fine," I say. "Have it your way."

I stand up, but she stops me.

"It's my mom," she says. "She has it in her head that I need riding and tennis lessons."

"And?"

"And so she's scheduled one for tomorrow. A riding lesson. Which means that not only did I have to miss the dance tonight, but I have to miss my soccer game tomorrow."

"I thought you didn't care about the dance. You know, all that talk about it being misogynistic or whatever."

"I don't care about the dance. But I care about my soccer game." Tears are staining her face. I reach over and awkwardly rub her back a bit. I can't help but feel a little sorry for her. "And actually, I do kind of care about the dance."

"But you said it was an archaic mating ritual or something."

"I just said that so people wouldn't know I wanted to go." She grabs a tissue off the side table and blows her nose. "Scarlett, I'm sorry for what I did to you. I don't know what I was thinking. I wasn't in my right mind."

My first instinct is to yell at her, but then I realize I haven't been in my right mind either.

"Why would you do it, though? I mean, I haven't done anything to you."

"I know," she says. *Sniff, sniff.* "I was upset. I broke up with James, and my mom was all 'You need to get back with him, Crissa, he's a wonderful boy' and then Marissa moved, and I was working my butt off in summer school, and then you just waltzed in here, out of nowhere, all flashy and sparkly. You seemed like you didn't have a care in the world." She blows her nose again, and then throws the tissue against the wall.

"I wasn't all flashy and sparkly," I say.

"Scarlett, you made a belt for your uniform out of a blue glitter headband." Hmm. Good point.

"But you knew I left my old school because of a big scandal," I say.

"Yeah, but you didn't seem affected by it," she says. "And I couldn't figure it out. Here I was, getting rattled about every little thing, while meanwhile, you were acting like you didn't have a care in the world. It didn't seem fair. I just . . . I dunno, I wanted to rattle you."

"How'd you know about my dad anyway?" I ask, looking down at my hands.

"My mom," she says. "When you applied to come to school here, your case got taken before the board."

"Oh." Jeez. That must have been some scene. All the board members considering whether or not I should be let into this school. I should have known it would be impossible to keep the thing about my dad a secret.

"And I was just so stressed out, so when James told me

his secret pen pal was new, I figured out it was you," she says. "And so I decided to mess with you. I'm really sorry."

I feel myself starting to get mad again, but then I sigh. "It's okay," I say. "I haven't been in my right mind either. Running around, doing all those crazy things, getting suspended."

"I can't believe you did them," she says. She looks down at her hands, and a little bit of a smile crosses her lips. But not in a mean way. More of a *Wow, you're not scared of anything* kind of way. "I never thought you'd actually go through with them."

"Me neither," I say. We sit there for a second, not saying anything, and then Miss Cardanelli appears at our door.

"Hey," I say, "what's going on?" I figure she's just bored and making rounds, trying to see if there's anyone left in the dorm.

"Scarlett," she says. "You have a visitor."

"I do?"

"Yes," she says. "I think your cousin. James?" I wait for her to mention that since I'm in trouble, I'm not allowed to have visitors, but she just gives me a wink. I don't realize I'm holding my breath until I let it all out. "He's down in the lobby with Amber and her date."

"Thanks," I say.

"You should talk to him," Crissa says once Miss Cardanelli's headed back down the hall. "All he can talk about is how cool you were, and how he didn't want to go along with my little scheme."

"Really?"

"Yeah," she says. "I knew you must have figured it out somehow, and I figured he was just going along with it because you told him not to stop. He's not a bad person."

"And you two are . . ." I wonder how to phrase it. Broken up? Just friends? Not interested?

"We're completely over," she says. "We've been over. In fact, I'm not sure we even really liked each other that much in the first place." She sighs and lays back down on her bed, looking up at the ceiling. She's stopped crying, but her eyes are still watery. "I mean, we've just always kind of been thrown together, you know? Ever since we were little kids."

"Yeah," I say.

"Anyway, you should talk to him," she says.

"Thanks," I say, giving her hand a squeeze. "And maybe when I come back we can talk about some ways to deal with your mom." Crissa smiles. I guess if Amber and my mom can give me a second chance, it can't hurt to give someone else one.

❈ ❈ ❈

I don't even bother to put on any makeup or change my clothes. I rush downstairs in my red pajama pants and black fleece top. And when I get down to the lobby, Amber, James, and a guy I don't recognize are sitting on one of the squashy couches in the common room.

"Hey," Amber says. "We figured since you couldn't come to the dance, we'd bring the dance to you. Well, as much as we could, anyway." She holds up a bottle of fruit punch. "This is all we managed to steal."

"That's okay," I grin, reaching for the bottle and taking a sip.

"This is Louis," she says, indicating the guy sitting next to her.

"Nice to meet you," Louis says, standing up to shake my hand. He's short, with wire-rimmed glasses, but he has a friendly-looking face.

"Nice to meet you, too," I say, and grin at Amber. And then I turn to look at James.

"Hey," he says shyly.

"Hey," I say. He moves over on the couch and I slide in next to him. We don't say anything for a second. Amber and Louis are down on the other side of the long couch. I can't really hear what they're saying, but it sounds like Louis is talking about some kind of ant farm, and Amber's giggling like it's the funniest thing she's ever heard. I guess she's open to bug flirting after all.

"Look, Scarlett," James starts. "I know that—"

I hold my hand up to stop him. "It's okay," I say. "I don't want you to say anything."

He frowns. "You don't want me to say anything because you're mad and you hate me, or because you're forgiving me?"

"I don't want you to say anything, because I want to start over," I say. I take a deep breath. "Just me and you. Not through writing stranger letters, not while I'm trying to manipulate my way through some dumb game, but just while we're trying to be ourselves."

He looks relieved. "I was hoping we could do that, but then you started sending me all those blank notes, and I know my apology doesn't necessarily mean that much, but—"

"It's okay," I say. I pull my feet up on the couch and curl them under me. I want to tell him that Crissa told me it wasn't his fault, that he really was looking out for me the whole time. But it's not about Crissa. It's just about James and me. "Let's just pretend we don't know each other. . . . So?" I say. "What's your favorite book, James?"

"*The Catcher in the Rye*," he says. And then he smiles and reaches his hand out and wraps it around mine.

❀ ❀ ❀

Monday morning in English, Miss Cardanelli announces that we're going to be writing to our secret stranger pen pals. And then I realize that I don't really have a secret stranger pen pal. I know James pretty well, especially after Friday night, when we stayed in the common room until midnight, when his bus left for BAFB, talking, laughing, and holding hands.

But I write him a note anyway.

Dear James,

I had fun Friday night at the "dance." I'm sure that by the time you read this, we'll have already talked on the phone.

Talk soon,
Scarlett

And then, since the rest of the class is still writing their letters, I decide I should write another one. The one I should have been writing all along.

I pull out a fresh piece of paper.

Dear Dad,

How are you? Sorry I have not written or called, but things have been crazy. Things at my new school are good. I'm on the basketball team; did Mom tell you? It's going okay so far. Anyway, I was wondering if maybe you wanted to come and visit soon? I'd like to show you the school and introduce you to my friends.

Let me know.

Love,
Scarlett

I reread the letter, then put it in an envelope and seal it. It's not much, but it's a start. And if there's anything I've learned lately, it's that everyone deserves a fresh start and a second chance. I lean back in my seat and wait for everyone else to finish.

❤ Acknowledgments ❤

Thank you, thank you, thank you to:

Molly McGuire, for taking this book all the way to Atlanta with her, and for her fabulous editorial guidance.

Kate Angelella, for taking over with such enthusiasm, and not laughing at me when I told her the story of how I almost-not-really became a soccer player.

Alyssa Eisner Henkin, for being everything I've ever wanted in an agent, and never being too busy to give me fab NYC restaurant suggestions.

My mom, for always being there no matter what, and setting an example for the kind of person I want to be.

My dad, for reading every single one of my books, even though he's totally not my target audience.

Krissi and Kelsey, for making me laugh, being the best sisters anyone could ask for, and making me proud of the young women they're becoming.

Kevin Cregg, for putting up with my craziness on an almost-daily basis for the past eleven years.

My new in-laws, the Gorvines, for being a "reading family" and always getting excited about my books.

My grandparents, for being proud of me and bragging about my books to everyone and anyone who will listen.

And most of all, everyone who read The Secret Identity of Devon Delaney and sent me an e-mail or Myspace message to let me know they loved it. You guys are awesome!